# The Veiled Vixen

# The Veiled Vixen

## Virginia Bown

**Walker and Company**
**New York**

First published in the United States of America in 1992 by
Walker Publishing Company, Inc.

Published simultaneously in Canada by Thomas Allen & Son
Canada, Limited, Markham, Ontario

Library of Congress Cataloging-in-Publication Data
Bown, Virginia
The veiled vixen / Virginia Bown.
p.    cm.
ISBN 0-8027-1189-8
I. Title.
PS3552.O87635V4   1992
813'.54—dc20        91-41493
CIP

Printed in the United States of America

2   4   6   8   10   9   7   5   3   1

# The Veiled Vixen

# 1

"But, Papa, I have no wish to marry the Marquess of Brodhurst," Lady Alicia announced, trying with only a modicum of success to retain her composure. "Such an alliance is unthinkable. I shall not agree." She raised her firm, although decidedly feminine, Granville chin and stood in quiet defiance of her father's words, her calm demeanor totally belying the inner turmoil she was experiencing.

Layton Granville, the fifth Earl of Wynford, usually agreeable to any of his beloved daughter's wishes, and in the past easily swayed by her arguments, was this time steadfast in his decision. "Nevertheless, Alicia," he replied firmly, "marry him you will." His own chin jutted out in response to her challenge of parental authority. "Arrangements have already been made. The marquess will call on you within the week. You will accept his offer."

Alicia fought to keep her voice calm. "I shall, of course, receive him with civility. As your daughter I could do no less. Marriage to him, however, is another matter entirely. I do not choose such an alliance."

The earl's complexion turned a shade darker as he listened to his daughter's reply. "Choose?" he questioned, the volume of his voice increasing with every word. "You defy my wishes, preferring to choose?" He glowered at her. "Very well. Choose then, and be quick about it. Name the man. Put an end to this matter here and now. If not the marquess, then who?"

Alicia bit her lip in dismay. There was no one she could possibly choose. The only eligible gentlemen in the area were either deadly bores or of the same age as her father. She shook her head sadly. "I have no one in mind, as yet."

"Ah hah! Thought as much." The earl slapped his thigh in satisfaction. "Just as well. Shouldn't care to give my consent to anyone around here. Poor lot, I'd judge. Knew you'd be of the same mind." He smiled at her, his color fading to near normal. "Come now, Allie, you're a sensible girl. It's time you made a match."

Alicia, hoping that her father's resolution was softening, voiced her appeal in gentler tones. "Is it so imperative that I marry now?" she queried with a shy smile. "May I not stay with you yet a while longer?"

The earl, truly devoted to his daughter and moved by her entreaty, took her hand, and patted it gently. "Pleases me you want to stay, Allie. Makes me proud." He hesitated, dropped her hand, and cleared his throat. "But it just won't do. A fine marriage is what you deserve, and I mean to see that you get it."

"But is there not still time for me to find someone with whom I might form an attachment?" she continued, pleading shyly with wide, innocent eyes.

He cocked his head, eyeing Alicia quizzically. "Do you fancy another Season in London, my dear? Is that why you dislike this arrangement so much?"

"Oh, no, not at all," she assured him quickly, hoping the anxiety his words had evoked did not evidence itself in her voice. She was in no hurry to repeat the disaster of her first visit to London.

"Just the same," the earl continued, "I've no doubt the city holds more excitement for a young girl than the quiet life we lead in the country."

"But I love it here, Papa. London holds no enchantment for me. I find contentment with you and Aunt Matilda. I don't wish to leave."

"Tsk, tsk. Only natural to have some reluctance, my dear. Understandable. This is the only home you've known. I can't fault you for being slow to leave. But leave you must. You'll get over it in time. All girls do. Brodhurst will help."

The mere mention of the marquess elicited a small sigh of exasperation. The earl's eyebrow arched at the sound, but he continued calmly. "You must begin to live your own life, daughter. Marriage and children. These are your future." He lowered his gaze, uncomfortable with the somewhat awkward turn the conversation had taken. He cleared this throat and started again.

"I have no wish to see my only child pass her life as a spinster. A marriage has been arranged. A good one. You will be more than comfortable, I've seen to that."

"But I do not wish to marry Lord Brodhurst, Papa. I am persuaded we cannot possibly suit. Such a match will only bring unhappiness to us both." she clasped her hands tightly as she held her head high and boldly faced her father. "No. I shall not marry him."

The earl stood quietly for a moment, his Granville chin becoming more apparent as he contemplated her statement. When he finally spoke, his voice was firm.

"This is a good match. I've done right by you. The man has a good family background. Knew his father well. There is no better match to be found. Give up the fight, Allie. You will marry the marquess."

The earl's inflexibility was surprising. Seldom had he ever denied Alicia anything. As a result, she could not calmly accept his decision without first exhausting every possible means of dissuasion. Her mind searched for acceptable arguments.

"But Papa, surely there must be some other . . ."

The earl shook his head. "You shall marry Brodhurst. I wish to hear nothing more on the subject."

Alicia felt her self-restraint slip at the earl's summary dismissal. The defiant young lady, facing her unusually stern parent, suddenly felt quite the schoolroom miss. "Oh, Papa, how could you!" she cried out, unable to contain her emotions further. With trembling lips and moist eyes, she ran from the room.

The earl, somewhat nonplussed by his daughter's head-long flight from his presence, could only stand and stare at the open door through which she had disappeared.

Alicia quickly gained the sanctuary of her own room, her bosom heaving from anxiety as well as the exertion of running up the long flight of stairs. Most certainly she needed to think clearly. Matters were serious. She had always known that her father expected marriage to be a part of her future, but somehow she had thought of such an event as taking place in the far distant future. Suddenly, however, in the few moments it had taken her father to inform her of the approaching betrothal, time had telescoped, and the future was now. What's more, she most definitely disliked having no say whatsoever in the shape her destiny was to take.

Marriage, with its accompanying surrender of all her personal freedom and wealth, was more than a little abhorrent to her independent spirit. If possible, she must find a means of extricating herself from the entanglement in which her father, with what she believed was a mistaken sense of benevolent parental duty, had placed her.

Feeling the need for a brisk ride to clear her mind, she summoned Mary, her maid, and proceeded to change into a forest green velvet riding habit, having first sent word to the stables to have her mare, Starfire, saddled and brought around.

Hurriedly descending the gently curved grand stairway, she quietly slipped out the front door to find the lively roan prancing impatiently as Thomas, the groom, held her in readiness for her ladyship's appearance. His own mount, a less spirited bay, waited quietly by the post.

"Gently, Starfire, we shall soon be on our way."

At the sound of Alicia's soft salutation, the mare steadied, allowing her mistress to mount without difficulty. "I wish to ride alone, Thomas," the young lady announced, taking the reins from the hands of the disapproving groom.

"But m'lady, 'tis not right that ye should go alone." The worried young man looked hesitantly toward his own horse. But his deep adoration of the Lady Alicia, coupled with the enchanting smile she bestowed upon him, finally resulted in his acquiescence. This was not the first time her ladyship had requested and received such freedom.

Soon both horse and rider, unaccompanied by proper escort, were galloping across the open fields of the Wynford estate. Alicia drank deeply of the familiar odor of damp horsehair and leather, enjoying an aroma which many young ladies of her breeding and position would consider less than agreeable. The rhythm of the hoofbeats seemed to say, "get away, get away, get away." They drummed into her thoughts as Alicia bent low and urged her mount on.

"Oh, I do wish so very much that I could get away," she whispered to Starfire.

Somehow she had never expected her father would actually do such a thing—finding her a husband indeed! She didn't desire a husband. The life of a spinster held no fears for her. On the contrary, if truth be told, such an existence held a great deal to recommend itself to one whose handsome inheritance would grant her a life of comfort and ease. And if she *did* ever decide to marry, she was perfectly capable of finding an eligible *parti* herself without parental help. Most certainly she would not choose the Marquess of Brodhurst! He was far too aware of his own consequence for her taste.

Lady Alicia allowed her long flaxen tresses to stream backward in the wind. In her extreme haste to leave the manor, she had forgone the usual hat and veil. It did not signify, however, for no one was around to see her.

She rode by instinct, letting her mind wander as she gloried in the power of the beloved animal beneath her. Her large blue eyes and fair complexion were accented by cheeks stung into glowing color from the bite of the early spring air. The charming effect was marred somewhat by the way her slim brows were wrinkled together in a small frown of worry.

Certainly she was aware that her first London Season had been less than a complete success. Disastrous might be a better term. She had been one of those unfortunates termed "late bloomers," and at seventeen, she had appeared rather angular, lacking in the curves and feminine graces so necessary for acceptance and approval. She had seemed miserably plain among the bevy of young ladies enjoying their first Season that year.

After certain catastrophic attacks on her self-esteem, she had returned to the Wynford estate and devoted herself to the country life she dearly loved. For two years, she had managed to avoid embarking upon another Season, and was still reluctant to enter the social whirl again.

Her father, unfortunately, had other ideas. He was well aware her chances of finding a suitable husband in the country were greatly diminished, and knew time to be definitely against her. He had no inkling that she was reluctant to marry at all. She could be perfectly content living out her life at Wynford Manor. Such an unfettered existence tempted her greatly.

She coaxed Starfire into a racing gallop, as if expecting to escape from her problems on the back of a horse. The bright sun was almost blinding, but most welcome after more than two weeks of gray skies and drizzle. The air was crisp and clean, and Alicia breathed it deeply, hoping to clear her mind.

The mare reached the edge of the woods at the south end of the estate, and since her mistress was too preoccupied to notice, slackened her pace as she entered the trees. Still deep in thought, Alicia urged her mount to greater speed.

The agile roan crashed through the underbrush, dodging trees and stumps. Her rider, finally awakening to the danger, pulled back on the reins to stop the headlong rush. Too late! Alicia spied the low hanging limb and jerked her horse to the left, ducking only a moment before her head could make contact. She escaped what might have been a most painful blow, but the movement forced Starfire into a thicket. The roan mare extricated herself and her mistress, but it was immediately clear she was quite lame.

After moments that seemed more like hours to Alicia, both horse and rider broke into the sunshine. Her ladyship brought the mare to a halt and dismounted. With more than a little trepidation, she gently examined the roan's left foreleg and found it hot to the touch and already badly swollen. It needed attention immediately.

Unfortunately no one lived near enough to help, but she remembered a nearby stream. Surely its cool water would help the swelling. She patted the sweat-streaked neck of her beloved roan, whispering words of apology and encouragement as they walked, tears of remorse threatening to cascade down her cheeks.

Silently she chastised herself for being so foolish as to let her mind wander while riding at such a breakneck pace. She accepted full responsibility for the incident and suffered greatly from the knowledge that she had caused the injury to her beloved mare.

The noon sun warmed her face as she led the injured roan carefully over the uneven turf. Unfortunately, it took longer than she had expected to reach the stream and she soon regretted having left her hat at home.

Finally, she heard running water and quickly found a place where the bank sloped gently. She carefully coaxed Starfire down into the rushing water and watched as the mare eagerly bent to drink.

Kneeling to wet a small hankie, she pressed its soothing coolness against her own hot temples as she sat down on the bank to rest.

The roan, having drunk her fill, whinnied softly and made to leave the stream. Alicia, attempting to quiet the animal, stood at Starfire's head, speaking softly and offering words of encouragement. She could not, however, induce the animal to remain quietly standing in the cold water.

Perhaps it was just as well, she decided, since she was not certain how such a prolonged soaking might affect the mare's health. As an alternative, she tore a ruffle from her petticoat and wet it thoroughly, then wrapped it around the injured leg and tied it securely. She could think of nothing more to do except see to it that Starfire had the best of care when they returned to Wynford Manor. Leading her limping mount, Alicia began the long trek home.

Upon her return to the manor, Alicia led the mare to the stables and sought out Thomas, explaining what had happened. After receiving assurances that her beloved mare would receive proper care, she slowly trudged up the gentle hill to the main house. She then entered by the garden door, attempting to reach her room unobserved, for she knew she must look a fright. She was forced, however, to slip into the library to avoid being seen by one of the footmen. Luncheon had passed without her presence, and the earl was loudly voicing his displeasure at his daughter's absence to his sister, Lady Matilda Ludlow, in the next room.

Alicia generally disdained eavesdropping, but she was well aware that anything her father might say could have a definite bearing on her future. Thus she allowed her curiosity to win out over better judgment. Tiptoeing over to the connecting door, she leaned close to listen.

"Dash it all, Mattie. This is just too bad of Alicia. Don't hold with pouting. Never believed she'd have a fit of temper about this marriage business. Humph! Thought I brought her up better than that."

"Now, Layton," Lady Matilda soothed, "don't be so harsh on the girl." The widow had been a member of the Granville household since Alicia's mother, the countess, died almost ten years ago. At that time the earl needed a hostess, and his young child needed someone besides a governess to help guide her into maturity. Lady Matilda fitted the bill exactly. Her husband had been killed in a hunting accident only a few months before the countess's death. The grieving brother and sister had gravitated together through natural affinity and had enjoyed the arrangement ever since. Matilda had a calming effect on her brother, and he always gave her a sense of being secure and needed.

"Let her sort things out alone, dear brother. I'm persuaded she'll come around in time. You probably weren't too tactful with the news."

"Dashed poor at beating 'bout the bush, as you well know," the earl retorted. "Just announced I'd found her a reasonably good husband, and that he'd be here to do the proper in a few days."

"Announced that *you'd* found her a husband?" Astonishment was evident in Matilda's voice. "Oh, the poor dear. She must be in quite a fret. Couldn't you at least have hinted that Brodhurst was interested in her, or had requested her hand?"

"Mattie, you know well enough she'd have learned different in a fortnight or less," Lord Wynford responded defensively. "She's no featherbrain. No sense raising the gel's hopes. The hurt's much worse when she's cut down. Best feed her the truth from the start, I'd say."

"The truth!" Lady Matilda gasped. "Oh, surely you didn't tell her of his reputation?"

Upon hearing that statement, Alicia smiled wryly, remembering the gossip which had been prevalent while she was in London. She doubted that her father could tell her anything about Lord Brodhurst which she hadn't already heard many times.

"Had better sense than to pass on gossip," the earl continued. "Brodhurst's a good man, just had a bit of a wild youth. Must admit he's a trifle too starchy and puffed up for my taste. But he's ready to settle down now. He'll do right by my Allie. Discreet and all that after the marriage. He promised, by Jupiter! She'll have the position and respect she deserves!"

Much I care for position, Alicia thought. She was a romantic at heart and inwardly acknowledged a preference for a man's adoration over society's respect.

"Yes, and he'll have her money," Lady Matilda retorted as she sipped her tea. "Layton, I can't help feeling you've invited a wolf to carry off our little lamb."

"Lamb? Hardly think so," the earl commented. "Unplumbed depths there, you know. The gel's got spirit, or so Brodhurst will find out in good time. Best thing that ever happened to either of them. Best thing all around." He trailed off, and Alicia could picture him nodding agreement with his own statement, as was his wont.

"Well, Layton, I'm sure you know best," Lady Matilda said. "After all, she is your daughter. But I fear the road you've chosen for her has a few ruts in it."

Alicia heard movement and feared she might be discovered. She quickly left the library and, after checking the corridor carefully for the presence of any of the staff, quietly slipped up the back staircase. She attained her room unobserved and gratefully sat down on the bed with a sigh of relief. Her eavesdropping had not resulted in her obtaining any information which might be helpful, and the hours she had spent in the blazing sun were making her head ache miserably. Without calling her maid, she undressed and crawled into bed. Closing her eyes against the pain, she fell asleep almost immediately.

She was woken by her maid, Mary, shrieking. Confused, she started to sit up in order to question her, but Mary ran from the room, exclaiming, "Oh, my heavens! Oh, my stars!"

"What has gotten into you?" Alicia asked the empty room.

"Alicia, my dear, what on earth has happened?" Lady Matilda swept into the bedroom. She spied Alicia's face and gasped. "Oh, good gracious! Whatever could have happened to your face, dear? You look positively horrid!"

Instinctively touching her cheeks, Alicia felt their extreme warmth. "Do I have a fever?" she asked as she hurried out of bed to the mirror. The reflection in the glass was that of a near-stranger with flaming red face and puffy eyes. The shock of her appearance stunned her for a moment. Then the events of the day flashed through her mind, and she knew what must have happened. The cause of her problem was quite simple. "Oh, Aunt Matilda," she exclaimed. "I'm dreadfully sunburned! Whatever am I going to do?"

"That's absurd. How could you possibly be burned? A lady never goes outside without a hat and veil. Still, you do have such delicate skin. . . . I have reminded you more times than I care to count of the need to take great care to protect your face from the sun and never to go out in the middle of the day. Surely you did not spend an excessive amount of time in the sun today?"

Alicia reluctantly nodded. She had no choice but to confess the details of the unfortunate incident which resulted in the injury to her mount. With downcast eyes, she also admitted to having gone riding without even the protection of hat or veil. "But surely I must have been in the sun for no more than three hours," she said.

"Well, my dear, whatever the time or amount of exposure, it appears to have been sufficient to have caused considerable damage to your complexion."

Alicia nodded her agreement as she turned to look again at the offending image in the mirror.

Without uttering another word, Aunt Matilda took charge of the situation, helping her niece to bed and sending Mary down to the kitchen. She soon returned with a cloth and a bowl of milk and tenderly applied poultices to her mistress's scarlet face. Alicia relaxed as the ministrations began to ease her discomfort.

"If you please, my Lady," Mary said, "Cook has a special salve."

"Excellent," said Aunt Matilda. "I've never known one of her remedies to go amiss. You had better stay upstairs for the rest of the day, my dear."

Alicia had no objections. All she wanted to do was rest.

The next morning found Alicia feeling much better— well enough, in fact, to leave her bed. She settled herself comfortably in the downstairs morning room and began working on her sampler.

The room was cheery, done in pale yellow and soft green, with cream and yellow striped satin covering the chairs and sofa. The drapes were open, but fortunately no sunshine streamed in; it was a cloud-covered day, gray and cheerless.

Alicia's apparel matched the weather. She was dressed warmly, if somewhat shabbily, in a faded brown dress with frayed white cuffs and collar. An old black shawl draped over her shoulders completed the drab picture.

Lady Matilda, pleased to hear that her niece was on the mend, quickly joined her. Dressed in a soft blue dimity frock, she was a sharp contrast to the sad picture presented by Alicia. As she entered the room, her mouth opened in astonishment.

"Goodness, what a dowd you present, my dear. I know you're feeling poorly, but must you wear such old clothes? I daresay that dress is straight from your days at Miss Wentworth's school. I'm persuaded you'd feel much better in a more stylish outfit." She sat down in an adjoining chair. Before she could begin her own needlework, however, she looked about the room, sniffing daintily. "And what is that peculiar odor?"

Alicia gingerly shook her head. "Cook's salve. The odor is horrible and seems to cling to whatever I wear. And what's more, if even the smallest amount gets on my clothes, it leaves a stain impossible to remove. That's why I'm wearing this old dress."

Matilda wrinkled her nose in distaste. "Very well. Have it so, if you must. But I've always held that convalescence is a time to wear one's prettiest lounging gowns, to be petted and cosseted, and made to feel loved and appreciated. It's absolutely the only thing which makes illness bearable."

She sighed and made to rise from her chair. "Pray excuse me for a moment, my dear. I'm persuaded that my own gown may absorb that abysmal odor of your salve, and I favor it too much to wish it such a fate. Perhaps one of my gardening gowns might be just the thing. I plan to join your father later in the greenhouse, anyway."

Lady Matilda returned some minutes later, this time

dressed more in keeping with the style forced upon her niece, namely an ancient brown muslin morning gown.

She once again settled herself in a chair near Alicia and picked up her needlework. "Now, my dear, let us have a comfortable coze. But perhaps we should not discuss fashion, for I'm persuaded anything which might remind us of our present costumes would serve only to depress us further."

Alicia laughed softly at her aunt's pronouncement. "Aunt Matilda, you're such a dear. How sweet of you to cheer me up. I haven't laughed since . . . since I was informed of my forthcoming betrothal." With the last distasteful words out of her mouth, she frowned her annoyance over the entire situation. The wrinkling of her baked skin was decidedly uncomfortable. "Oh dear, how vexing," she exclaimed. "It hurts to smile or to frown, and I find it difficult to keep neutral and do neither."

"Perhaps it's for the best, my dear. This will be good practice for you. A lady should keep a calm and pleasant expression as much as possible. Equanimity of face and thought is to be prized, believe me. And as a married lady, you will be expected to act with more composure and decorum than you have shown in the past."

Lady Alicia raised her Granville chin in defiance. "I've not yet decided I shall be married!" Her aunt's words only enhanced her belief that marriage would require the surrender of every vestige of independence. She would prefer to forgo such a situation, at least until she was truly in love. That love might render the state of matrimony bearable, she had no doubt, but the well-regulated affection that she had been taught was the foundation of a stable and happy marriage did not seem inducement enough for her to choose to forfeit her freedom. To her, however, the most practical choice would be no marriage at all.

She was used to having her own way. Her father could be autocratic, but with a little daughterly cajoling his will could usually be bent to coincide with her own. Most of the time, she felt no restraints upon her life whatsoever. But this time she chafed under her father's determination to arrange his daughter's future. She tapped her foot in exasperation. "Papa has moved too quickly. I'm not considered on the shelf yet. There's still time to find someone of my own choosing."

Lady Matilda picked up her sewing, deftly working her needle as she spoke. "That's the crux of the problem, dear. You haven't been looking at all. Besides, my brother has definitely not moved quickly. On the contrary, he has shown great restraint. You see, this marriage was planned by your parents years ago. You were just a babe at the time. Neither you nor Lord Brodhurst was told." She stopped and looked up at her niece with a sad smile, then continued.

"It was hoped that the two of you would meet when you made your debut. The earl was of the belief that it was a match made in heaven, and that you would find each other—perhaps fall in love. Unfortunately, it didn't happen." A small sigh escaped her lips as she returned to her work. "Poor Layton. He was so disappointed."

That her father knew she would be loath to accept a marriage based on a business agreement brought little comfort to Alicia. And most assuredly she did not want to do business with the marquess. She needed something more. She wanted love, and it would be difficult in the extreme for her unrestrained spirit to accept the constraints of an arranged marriage when she had not yet had a proper chance to find that elusive passion. Yet, in all honesty, Alicia had to accept a great part of the blame for the predicament in which she found herself. She should have returned to London instead of retreating to the safe premises of her father's estate.

Thoughts of her disastrous Season greatly discomfited Alicia. She disliked recalling her days in London; some of the memories were still quite painful. She pulled the shawl snugly about her shoulders as if to ward off a sudden chill. Then, with a determined set to her features, she began to relate something she had never before disclosed. "Father's plan did succeed . . . in part. The marquess and I did meet, Aunt Matilda. His lordship was introduced to me three times."

"Three times?" Matilda repeated, questioningly. "How very astonishing. I've never heard of such a thing. How could it possibly have happened? Lord Brodhurst has never been known to act so uncivil."

"Oh, I'm persuaded the cut was not intentional," Alicia replied, then hesitated. "Or at least I don't believe so. The case was more likely that he simply didn't remember me."

"That's quite possible. To a man accustomed as he is to a succession of routs and receptions, forgetting a previous introduction is understandable. But to forget a second time?" Lady Matilda shook her head slowly. "You poor dear, how very mortifying!"

Alicia stopped her aunt from further expressions of condolence with a wave of her hand. "It was quite understandable. I was such a mouse, and so terribly gawky. He was handsome and charming, and of course most eligible. All the girls and their mamas were trying to catch him. I was merely lost in the crush."

"Alicia, my dear, I do so wish you had confided this to me earlier. No wonder you were overwrought by the news of your betrothal. Your father unwittingly has put you in an intolerable position. No lady desires to marry a man who appears to feel she is beneath his notice. To be actively disliked is preferable to that! Your father must be told. Perhaps it is not too late."

Alicia glumly nodded her concurrence. "That the marquess should agree to this marriage is puzzling in the extreme. I had the distinct impression that the mere thought of marriage was abhorrent to him. But perhaps that was only the thought of marriage to me."

Lady Matilda placed her work on the table and clasped her hands as if to begin a schoolroom lecture. "Well, it's not so abhorrent to him now. When his father died last year and he assumed the title, it became apparent that marriage was his duty. The line must have an heir. If not, his cousin inherits, and there's much bad blood on that side of the family. Not only must he take a wife, she needs be an heiress as well. And, my dear, he would have had no reason at the time to think of you as his bride. Remember, he, too, knew nothing of your parents' plans."

"Is his family hard-pressed, then?" asked Alicia, clearly astonished at the news that Brodhurst wanted a wealthy wife.

"No, no, but his pockets are not as deep as they could be. Bad investments by his father over the years have depleted his capital somewhat. By marrying well, he could refurbish Brodhurst Manor and its lands, buy new stock, and put the farms back on a paying basis. So when your father informed him of the nuptial agreement between our families, he was surprised but quite amenable."

Before Lady Matilda could continue, Lord Granville appeared at the doorway. By his side was a tall gentleman of about thirty, whose black hair, piercing blue eyes, and firm jawline dominated his features. He was impeccably dressed in a dark green whipcord coat and cream-colored pantaloons. Gleaming Hessians completed the striking picture and seemed to underscore the earl's sorry attire. Lord Granville's eccentricities included his love of wearing comfortable but shabby clothes while at home in the country. It was clear to his daughter and sister that he had been happily puttering in the garden, which accounted for his raiment being in even worse condition than was his wont.

Paying no heed to the tears and smudges on his garments, the earl happily beamed as he ushered in the visitor, who carried himself with a grace unusual in a man so tall and long of leg.

"Ah, my dears, may I present Jonathan Bolton, Marquess of Brodhurst." His hand swept around toward his guest. "Brodhurst, my sister, Lady Matilda Ludlow, and my little Alicia."

The marquess bowed elegantly and stepped forward to take the proffered hands of the ladies.

"Matilda," Lord Granville called, "do join me for a moment. There's a matter of import we must discuss. I'm sure we may leave these two alone for a short time without compunction, don't you agree?" The earl accompanied his request with a conspiratorial wink.

Lady Matilda, quite flustered, arose and caught at her brother's sleeve in hopes of detaining him. "But Layton, dear, there's something you should—"

"Not now, Mattie. Be a good girl and come along." Firmly, the earl led his sister from the room.

"I'm relieved your father left us alone," the marquess said. "We have a great deal to discuss."

Alicia, who had kept her head lowered during the introductions out of confusion and nervousness, continued to stare down at her tightly clasped hands. She was well aware that the marquess had given no indication of having met her before. That's four, she thought, four times we've been introduced. Indignation began to overcome her timidity. Well, this time he's going to remember me, she vowed silently, and lifted her head to meet his gaze directly.

Lord Brodhurst had been eyeing her faded dress and ragged shawl in perplexity. Such shabby clothing was certainly not the usual attire of the ladies he normally attended and especially not of an heiress as decidedly plump in the pockets as the daughter of the Earl of Wynford was reported to be. Also, a dreadful odor had assailed his nostrils, slightly sour with a hint of herbs. It permeated the room but seemed to emanate from the young lady seated before him.

As she lifted her head, his mouth opened momentarily in astonishment. He had never before seen a lady with such a florid complexion. "She's red," he muttered to himself. "By Jupiter, she's absolutely red!"

Lady Alicia's face was vivid, a result of her anger as well as the sunburn. Puffy eyelids and an oily sheen completed the unpleasant picture.

From his earliest days, Lord Brodhurst had been trained in the discipline of good manners. There were few occasions when his aplomb had been even slightly shaken. But when he had been informed of the arrangement between the two families he had also been led to believe a bride near to his dream of perfection awaited him. What he saw now was more than even *his* poise could accept. He stepped back defensively as Alicia spoke.

"Are you aware that we have met three times previously?" she asked, her eyes flashing.

The marquess hesitated for a moment. Then, with a steely glint in his eye, he spoke. "You must be mistaken, dear lady. It would be impossible for me to forget such a vision." The distaste underlying his words was quite apparent.

Suddenly Alicia realized what a sad picture she presented. Her hands flew to her crimson cheeks involuntarily. Her eyes widened with the shock of humiliation. She attempted to regain some dignity.

"Lord Brodhurst, I do wish you will excuse my appearance. I was not expecting—prepared—for your visit." Her voice trailed off.

That fact was quite obvious to the gentleman. He sought in vain to find some reason for the strange condition of the lady before him. Doubtless he had been most grossly deceived. Not only was she lacking in comeliness to a most marked degree but also the state of her clothing proved Lord Wynford had quite misrepresented the family's financial status. As the marquess stared at the girl, he wondered at such perfidy, dumbfounded that the earl, a man respected in the highest circles, would have lent himself to such a scheme.

Anxious to leave the room under any pretext, he played upon the lady's discomfiture. "Since it is apparent that this is not the most propitious moment for our discussion, please allow me to take my leave, perhaps to return at a more convenient time."

Alicia was suddenly aware that, for the first time since she had made his acquaintance two years earlier, it was Lord Brodhurst who seemed to be nervous and unequal to the moment. Since she had been placed at a decided disadvantage by being forced to accept the attendance of this gentleman at a time when she must look an absolute fright, she was of the opinion it was true justice that someone else should suffer as well. A slight smile played at her lips as she decided to make a game of it.

"Oh, by no means, Lord Brodhurst. We could not allow you to leave without at least accomplishing the purpose for which you traveled so many miles. And as for my appearance, think nothing of it. We must be prepared to accept each other's eccentricities, don't you agree? Now, pray continue. You mentioned we have much to discuss?"

Nonplussed at her bold acceptance of her repellent appearance, the marquess concluded that Lady Alicia meant to press for a formal betrothal. The best course of action was obviously to continue his retreat. "Forgive my ill choice of words. I meant only to convey that perhaps the agreement between your father and I has been too hasty. Perhaps we should reconsider and discuss the matter sometime in the future."

"Do you wish to withdraw your offer?" she asked, coming directly to the point. His words had shocked her into abandoning the game and speaking forthrightly. She felt a perplexing pang of disappointment. Where was the expected pleasure which should be filling her bosom at the prospect of being relieved of the necessity of marrying the marquess?

Forced into speaking more bluntly, Brodhurst stared down at the red-faced girl seated before him. "I have not yet made an offer," he declared coldly.

"Oh!" Alicia's hand fluttered to her mouth. How lowering to be told such a thing by one's supposed betrothed. She glanced away in confusion.

Struck by her charming and surprisingly innocent re-action, he sought to comfort her. "Lady Alicia, I have no wish to cause you further embarrassment. Let us put an end to this entire affair. Now that I have exposed your scheme, let us say no more. I shall depart and speak of this to no one, provided, of course, that you and your father abandon any further attempts to ensnare me as your victim."

Alicia couldn't believe her ears. She rose slowly from

her chair, staring up at the marquess in shocked anger. "Scheme? Ensnare? Victim? Sir, these words are an insult. How could you be so impertinent, so vulgar, so—so ill-bred as to even think such things, let alone actually give voice to them?" Her eyes, as if reflecting her glowing cheeks, seemed to flash fire. "Are you implying—"

Stung by her speech, Brodhurst gave up trying to spare her any undue suffering. He decided to speak to her in a manner she could not misinterpret. "I am implying nothing, merely putting words to the obvious. Your father is apparently light in the pocket, and you are in need of a husband. It appears that I would be the answer to both your problems. The tale of my father agreeing upon a marriage pact was doubtless all a hum, meant only to entrap me."

His eyes grew dark and his voice took on a cutting edge. "Best you cast about in another direction for an eligible husband. It seems I shall not find a countess here." He bowed, turned on his heel, and walked out.

Tears of pain and frustration glistened on Alicia's cheeks as she stared at the empty doorway in shocked disbelief.

$$== 2 ==$$

"I'LL CALL HIM OUT, by God!" Lord Granville shouted as he paced in front of the yellow brocade chaise where Alicia reclined, a cold compress on her forehead.

She winced each time he spoke out loudly, but kept her eyes closed and said nothing. The events of the morning had resulted in another most disagreeable headache, and her father's ear-splitting reminder of the events which had transpired between her and the marquess did little to ease her pain. The most surprising result of the entire affair, however, was her inner confusion. To be sure she had been insulted, but by all rights she should be pleased to be free from the prospect of marrying Lord Brodhurst. Instead she tasted the bitterness of disappointment as well as the humiliation of rejection. She said nothing of her feelings, however, as her father continued to rant, unaware of her discomfort.

"Taste of steel, that's what he deserves! Better yet, a public thrashing! Damme, he'll not insult this family with impunity!"

Lady Matilda, who was long inured to her brother's warm language during times of extreme provocation, was not at all discomfited by his rantings and sat calmly sipping her tea from a delicate china cup as he paced the floor. She, too, was overset by the events of the morning, appearing pale and drawn in the afternoon light, but so far had remained quiet, as if unwilling, as yet, to add her voice to the general uproar.

The news of Lady Alicia's disastrous meeting with the marquess had spread quickly through the household. The daughter of the fifth Earl of Wynford was greatly loved by all who served her, and the entire staff was ready to take up arms and march against the house of Brodhurst in retaliation.

The earl himself appeared ready to lead the attack. He had seemed perilously close to apoplexy when told of the marquess's outrageous behavior, and in the hours since, had worked himself into a fine rage.

"Blast the man!" he fumed. "He's a bungler! A damned stiff-rumped fool! A blubberheaded idiot!" He stopped, worked his mouth as if to bring forth an even greater expletive, then exhaled and sat down in the nearest chair, appearing much like a deflated balloon.

His face slowly drained of some of its vivid color and he spoke to his daughter in a softer tone. "I'm the idiot, Alicia. Too impatient. Pressed too hard for the match. Too excited by that lout's visit to notice your appearance." He wiped his forehead and slowly shook his head. "But, damme, Allie, how could that cur possibly look at your gentle innocence and judge it guilty of such a scheme?"

"I don't know, Papa," she answered softly, wondering herself why the marquess would believe such a thing of her. She couldn't explain why her entire experience with Lord Brodhurst had been one of confusion, humiliation, and pain. Nothing ever seemed to go correctly when she was in his presence. She closed her eyes against the pain in her forehead but could do nothing to ease the dull ache centered in her bosom which accompanied it. If her father expected more of an answer from her, he was to be disappointed. She was too emotionally exhausted to join the discussion.

Aunt Matilda, however, broke her silence and slowly shook her lace-capped head as she spoke. "I own I don't know what could have possessed the man, Layton. I've asked myself the same question you just voiced, but there's no acceptable answer. Although his reputation as a rake is well known—" She hesitated, glancing quickly at Alicia to discover if her words had been too much of a shock for the young girl, then satisfied that they were not, continued. "Nevertheless, his treatment of Alicia is inexplicable. The man is a gentleman, and by all accounts, his manners have always been unexceptionable. But this morning—"

"This morning," the earl interrupted, "this morning the boor didn't wait for explanations. Didn't even *ask* for any. He must have been foxed to jump to that scurrilous conclusion. The insolent cub! Barbarian!"

Alicia winced with each word as her father began to warm up to his previous level of agitation. She could not help but feel a great load of guilt for all that had taken place. The responsibility for the entire affair could be traced to her actions of the previous day. It had been her own willfulness that had driven her to ride off alone, at such a breakneck speed. The injury to her beloved mare, the sunburn, and her subsequent unsightly appearance were all results of her headstrong act.

That her father's precipitous introduction of the marquess, with little or no consideration for his daughter's condition, should bear more than slight responsibility for the sad state of affairs was a fact which she refused to consider at the moment. Outside of her own guilt she could only acknowledge blame in the actions of Lord Brodhurst himself. However unfit her condition and appearance, there was no excuse for his behavior. His conclusions and abrupt withdrawal were nothing less than abominable. Guilt, anger, and humiliation combined to force a tear from beneath her closed lids, and she quickly dabbed at her eyes with a lace-edged handkerchief.

Matilda saw the telltale action and reached over to give Alicia a comforting pat on the arm before turning her attention to her brother, hoping to keep him from causing his daughter any further discomfort.

"Now Layton, don't get in another fret. Have some tea, dear. I'm persuaded it will do much to calm that temper of yours and clear your mind. We must consider the situation very carefully." She poured the tea gracefully and held out the cup to her brother. When he had reluctantly crossed the room to fetch it and seated himself in the empty chair beside her, she continued the conversation. "I'm wondering if perhaps there might be one plausible answer to this puzzle. Could it be possible that he did not want the match after all and used Alicia's awkward situation as an excuse?"

"An excuse?" Lord Granville sputtered, finding difficulty in swallowing the sip of tea he had just taken. "Are you saying that clod accused my daughter of duplicity just because he didn't have the backbone of a caterpillar? Balderdash! He may have lost his wits but not his courage!"

"No, no, Layton. I didn't mean that. Well, not exactly. But I do collect he may have felt somewhat chafed by the financial consideration which propelled him to his marriage. It's entirely possible that after rethinking the entire affair, he may have jumped at the first opportunity which presented itself to cancel the arrangement."

"Can't agree with you this time, Mattie. It just don't figure. If the boy had any reservations about the match, he would have mentioned them long ago. Had plenty of time to consider everything before he signed."

Alicia's eyes flew open. "Signed?" she whispered.

"Signed?" Lady Matilda repeated, her astonishment visibly apparent. "You mean the marquess actually signed a nuptial agreement?"

"Of course he did," the earl responded, placing his cup on the serving cart and smiling at the two women in smug satisfaction. "Wouldn't say so if he didn't. I'm no lackbrain. Made certain he did right by my Allie. She gets a fine jointure if he leaves her a widow. Worked it out in detail. The paper's binding. He can't back out."

"But that means Alicia is also bound!" Matilda exclaimed.

Alicia sat upright, allowing the compress to slide to the floor. "Oh, Papa, how could you!"

"Good gracious!" Matilda continued. "A pretty coil this

has become." Her remarkably unlined face worked itself into an unaccustomed frown.

Lord Granville grinned, clearly proud of his handiwork. "Wrong, sister dear. Trust me to have more sense." He strode to his daughter's side and took her hand gently. "Calm your fears, Allie. Knew there was a chance you would balk. Didn't really want to force you—just wanted your happiness. So there's a release clause. Gives you the right to cancel but not Lord Brodhurst." He was pleased to see the smile of relief on his daughter's face as he bent down to retrieve the fallen compress.

Matilda beamed her approval. "How good of you, Layton. That certainly changes everything. Well done, I must say."

"Humph! Yes, yes . . . ," the earl muttered in pleased embarrassment. "Good thing, too. Can't have Allie tied to a loose screw like Brodhurst. I'll have her sign the cancellation tomorrow. Good riddance, I'd say."

"Oh, Layton, I do wish you won't be so hasty. There's plenty of time for that. I own it may be best that you let the marquess stew a bit. He should pay a little for riding roughshod over our dear Alicia, don't you think?" She smiled reassuringly at her niece, who stared back in perplexity. "Perhaps he can be made to see the error of his ways, or at least to suffer a trifle for them. I'm persuaded his lordship should be taken down a peg—too toplofty by half, I'm thinking."

"Aunt Matilda!" Alicia exclaimed. "You're planning mischief. I can read it in your eyes."

"Perhaps, dear, perhaps." She smiled knowingly. "But I shall say no more on that head. I've a great deal to think on. Now, Layton, we should let this poor child have a little peace. We want her recuperation to be swift." With that pronouncement, she took her brother's arm and walked him to the door. She turned to Alicia just before leaving. "I'll come up to see you before dinner, dear." Go back to bed," she said, then escorted the earl out the door and closed it gently behind her.

Alicia wondered what her aunt was planning, but her

head hurt too much to think on it for long. She took the opportunity to rest. By evening she was sitting up in bed, munching on a piece of dry toast and sipping tea when her aunt knocked lightly on the door and peeked in.

"Oh, I'm so pleased you're feeling better, dear. Your father and I were worried when you didn't even take a sip of your tea earlier." She glanced at the tray disapprovingly. "I own it would be preferable to see you eat something a bit more nourishing, however."

"I'm sorry, Aunt Matilda, but I simply have no appetite. Mary practically forced this tray on me. She threatened to send for my old nurse if I didn't try to eat. Of course the mere thought of Morrow ringing a peal over me was terrifying!" Her blue eyes brightened with amusement. "She always was such a terrible scold. Even so, I do miss the dear tyrant a bit. Nonetheless, as you see, I yielded to Mary's demand."

She took another nibble of her toast before pushing the tray away with finality. "Enough! I can't possibly eat another bite."

Matilda raised an inquisitive eyebrow. "Well, I hope you can do better the next time. Perhaps you should plan to join us downstairs for dinner. Conversation always seems to spark my appetite, so perhaps it might have some beneficial effect on yours."

"Oh, no, I simply have no strength for that yet. Besides, I still need to keep my face covered with this odious salve. I simply could not face Papa at the dinner table looking such a fright, especially after this morning."

Alicia had been trying to avoid thinking about her undeserved set-down by the marquess. The mere mention of medicine, however, was enough to bring back every painful detail of the fiasco. She turned her head away, her vision having suddenly become quite blurred.

"Of course you mustn't come down until you're better. What a ninny I am to even suggest such a thing! What you need is lots of rest and no more worries. Put that little misunderstanding of this morning out of your head and just concentrate on getting well. It will all come about, my dear. I'm sure of it. Trust me. I have a plan and will speak more on the matter when you're feeling up to it." So saying, Matilda smiled confidently and patted her niece's hand. "I'll be back later."

Alicia sighed, lowering her head back into the soft feather pillow. Two small tears trickled down her cheeks. They were followed by more, and soon she was sobbing, yielding completely to the total humiliation and frustration she had experienced. Although not one to sink deeply into self-pity, she found it a relief to free the emotions she had kept imprisoned all day. Her wounded pride was bathed in a torrent of tears. Then, with a sniff, a small shudder, and a deep sigh, she sat up, feeling much better.

She recalled the hateful words spoken by the marquess. This time, however, the hurt and guilt were replaced by anger. She was furious at him for his accusation and exasperated at herself for her inability to counter with a skillful attack of her own. He was a conceited snob, so puffed up with his own consequence that he expected every young lady to resort to any means, fair or foul, to snare him. That he would include her in this gaggle of females constantly pursuing him was galling to say the least. He most certainly was in need of a good set-down, and she desperately wanted to be the one to give it to him. The Granville blood within her cried out for retaliation. But unused as she was to the social repartee practiced by the ton, any battle of words with his lordship would find her at a distinct disadvantage. There was only one way to acquire the needed skill. It was time to return to London.

The decision was made before she realized it. She'd neglected that part of her education far too long. She would have another Season, but this time she wouldn't be the shy and awkward little miss, too drab to be noticed. This time, she planned to shine and make the others look drab by comparison. So drastic a step, however, needed moral support. She hastened to her aunt's room, knocking lightly before entering the blue-flowered chamber.

Matilda was seated at her small escritoire. She smiled her welcome to Alicia, and then bent her head to continue the note she was writing.

"Aunt Matilda," Alicia began, "I have come to a decision of major proportions. We should journey to London as soon as possible. It's time I return."

Matilda looked up, completely unperturbed. "Yes, dear, you're very wise. In fact, our minds seem to have been working in unison, for at this very moment I am in the process of writing to your father's man of business, requesting that he arrange to open up Wynford House and make all the necessary arrangements for our journey to that august city."

"Oh, you are such a dear," Alicia exclaimed. "How could you have known I would want to go?"

"It's not a matter of knowing what you might desire but rather that you simply have no choice, my dear. You must present yourself to the ton and give lie to any false impressions the marquess might have spawned with a careless remark. And most certainly you must have a bit of revenge upon his lordship as well, don't you think?" Her soft brown eyes were twinkling again as she smiled up at her niece.

"I own it would be pleasant to cause him some discomfort in payment for the slights and cruel words he has given me and also to teach him not to humiliate another unsuspecting maiden. But how can such a thing be possible? You mentioned the signed pact earlier, but I confess to being much too distraught to attend your words fully. How could a nuptial agreement be used for our ends now?"

"Very simply, my dear. By informing the marquess that you will not cancel the agreement, you place him in an almost intolerable position. He has stated that he will not marry you, yet he remains bound by honor as well as by law to fulfill his promise. He will be most uncomfortable, I promise you."

"But I must remind you I don't wish to honor the agreement," Alicia argued, ignoring a strange feeling of sadness which settled upon her. "You know I have wished to be free of that odious gentleman from the moment I was apprised of the arrangement."

"And so you will be, but not until he has been made to squirm a little. When you feel that he has suffered enough, then you may send him your written cancellation and be finished with the entire affair. What do you say to my idea?"

Alicia pondered the suggestion for a moment. "It's perfect, Aunt Matilda, just perfect!" She gave the older lady a quick hug before returning to her room. Smiling to herself as she sat down before her mirror, she considered their plan of action. But first, she thought as she dabbed on some salve, her face must heal. She must be patient and give it time—a bit more time, she mused, continuing to apply the ointment gently to her tender skin.

She would have another Season, and this time it would be a triumphant one. Providence might intervene to the extent that she meet a gentleman with whom she could consider living the rest of her life. But any plans for the future must be set aside until her business with Lord Brodhurst was completed. He would pay for the suffering he had inflicted on her and her family. She promised herself a sweet revenge.

# = 3 =

LORD BRODHURST STOOD IN the library of Brodhurst Manor and poured himself a glass of brandy. He had changed his clothes since returning from the Wynford estate, and now wore a brown jacket of fine wool over a brocade waistcoat and pale yellow breeches. He blended very well with the fine old leather furnishings and deep mahogany bookcases of the exquisitely furnished, but decidedly masculine, room. Cream and gold embroidered draperies covered tall, narrow windows which looked out over gently sloping grounds leading down to a small, willow-framed lake that was ornamented with several graceful swans.

Beyond the lake lay open fields followed by a large stand of hardwood trees which served as a windbreak as well as to beautify the view. These trees, however, were hidden at the moment by a gray mist which shrouded the entire countryside. The marquess sipped his brandy and stared out the window at the bleak landscape. Since his return that afternoon the weather had worsened. The temperature had dropped and it was drizzling. "Matches my mood completely," he commented to himself, emptying the glass and letting the liquid warm him from within as it traveled down. Before he could refill his glass, Sir Edmund Coswell was announced, and the scowl on Lord Brodhurst's face was replaced by a smile as he turned to greet his houseguest.

Sir Edmund, although not as tall as his host, was still

an imposing figure as he strode across the room. He filled his coat of blue superfine to perfection, and his legs, covered by skintight beige-colored breeches, were very well formed for a man of his forty-three years.

Brodhurst clasped his friend's hand and led him over to the desk. "Sorry I wasn't here when you arrived, Edmund. I was attending to some very distasteful business." He gestured toward the decanter. "Join me in some brandy?"

Edmund happily nodded his assent, pleasure at seeing his friend quite evident in the broad smile which filled his round face. "Hope I didn't come at a bad time, Jonathan. You certainly didn't look too happy when I entered."

"No, no, glad you could come. In fact, your timing couldn't have been better. We shall celebrate together."

"Oh? Have you had some good news?" he questioned, accepting the proffered glass from his host.

"Hardly!" Brodhurst snorted. "No, today we shall celebrate my escape. A very narrow escape, I might add!"

"Good Lord! You've been imprisoned then?" Sir Edmund was aghast. He emptied his glass in one gulp. "Who's the scoundrel? Wait until I get my hands on him!"

"Now, now, my friend. Calm yourself." Brodhurst smiled and refilled Edmund's glass. "Your impatience to defend me is gratifying. But I assure you there's no need. I wasn't held prisoner, but rather very nearly trapped into a most unsuitable marriage. Got out just in time, I'll tell you. I shudder to think how close I came to being bamboozled into accepting that disfigured, impoverished female as my bride!" He finished his brandy and placed the crystal goblet on the tray.

"You've dodged many a snare in the past and never given it a thought, Jonathan. Why was this particular conspiracy so odious? Was she really so unsightly?"

"God! She was beastly! I swear she had some hideous disease. Her face was swollen and mottled, and she was positively red! Not a blush, mind you, but an overall red complexion. Ghastly!"

"Humph! Never heard of a disease like that." Edmund cocked his head and eyed his friend. "Are you certain there isn't more to this than a homely girl trying to trap you? It's not like you to be so upset. There's something you're keeping back. Out with it, man."

Jonathan faced the window and stared at the rain for a moment. Then, without looking at his guest, began to speak. "Edmund, I've never told a soul what I'm about to disclose to you now, and I do so only because of our many years of friendship. But I must have your promise not to repeat it."

"You have my word, old chap. Shouldn't have to ask, you know. I've always kept our conversations private. Usually do keep my mouth closed and my ears open."

"Sorry, my friend, but I feel so foolish about this whole affair, I'd hate to face White's if this got out." He looked down at his boots for a moment, then spoke softly. "This tangle really began about three years ago. I was making the usual round of parties and balls. There was one girl, barely out of the schoolroom. I own her exact features evade me now, but my impression at the time was that she was pretty. Shy, a sweet little thing—not a bit like all the simpering misses who were constantly giggling and following one about with their eyes. She was refreshing, and I saw to it that we were introduced, but after that she positively ignored me."

"Ignored you?" Edmund repeated. "You mean to say the gel gave you the cut direct in public?"

"Well, not exactly. I confess it didn't appear to be an intentional cut, but she never looked for me or tried to position herself close by. It was damned frustrating, I'll say."

"Oh ho! Don't tell me the great Brodhurst found a female who wasn't interested?" Edmund quickly placed his finger on his lips in a mock attempt to chastise himself for the near-chortle which had escaped. "Sorry, dear chap, couldn't help it. The laugh just slipped out. Go on, go on."

Jonathan raised an accusing eyebrow, then shrugged

and continued. "Well, I actually asked to have myself presented to her a second time, just to make certain she knew who I was. But damn it all, Edmund, she didn't blink an eye. I'll swear she'd forgotten our first introduction. Galling to say the least! She just smiled politely, but very coolly, and then turned back to her friends."

The older man's eyes twinkled with mirth. "Glad to hear there's still a female with some sense. Trouble is, Jonathan, you can be much too aware of your own consequence and expect too much. In addition, it's nigh to impossible to satisfy you. First you can't abide a chit who's constantly casting out lures. Then, when you meet one who doesn't seem to care, you're piqued."

"Damn right, Edmund. How would you like some chit to look down her nose at you upon first meeting? Then, shortly thereafter, forget your very existence."

Edmund rolled his eyes. "Pains me to admit to it, old man, but I've had that experience. And more than once I might add. Didn't much care for the feeling, I'll say. Still, I survived. It's not the end of the world, my friend."

"It may not be the end of the world, but it is certainly an insult I was not inclined to accept. A marquess should never be ignored or forgotten." His voice grew louder toward the end of the pronouncement.

"Ah yes, but I must call to your mind the fact that the title had not yet been bestowed upon you," Edmund calmly replied. "You had only yourself to rely on."

"True. But I was the heir, and my expectations were such that every female I met was duly impressed! I suppose I was rather conceited."

"Rather," Edmund said airily. "But tell me more about the lady."

The marquess nodded. A small muscle rippled in his cheek, as if he were intrigued by the memory of her audacity. "Naturally such impudence could not be allowed to go unrewarded. Therefore, I arranged to be presented to her again."

"A third introduction?" Sir Edmund raised an eyebrow.

"Yes," the younger man replied, "and that time she

remembered me. I could see it in her eyes. She was astonished when Lady Gosset began the introduction and tried to acknowledge our acquaintance. But I pretended to be unaware of any previous meeting. She followed my lead and played the game to the end, even curtsied nicely. But she was stung, that much was evident."

Edmond shook his head. "Devilish bad ton, Brodhurst. Did the chit really deserve such a severe cut?"

"I'll admit to some misgivings about the entire affair. I was ready to mend fences. Unfortunately she disappeared—left London and didn't return. And although our families do have a history of some slight acquaintance, I never saw her again."

"But you've been thinking about her all this time?"

Brodhurst shot a scathing glance toward his guest. "Hardly!" he said haughtily. "Females do not get that much of my attention. Least of all this particular young lady." He fought back the guilt which came with such a falsehood. Seldom had he kept anything from his good friend, but this was something he had difficulty acknowledging to himself, let alone telling another. How could he, in all seriousness, confess the thing which gave the entire incidence such importance? Namely, his unshakable feeling that she was more than just an interesting female, that she was special, that she might be the one who could fill the indescribable knot of loneliness within him. Being determined to control situations instead of being controlled by them, he had fought against the growing interest which drew him to her. And so, after she repaired to the country, he had refused to follow her.

Sir Edmund seemed to suspect there was more to his friend's reactions than had been revealed, but he declined to press the issue. "Have it your way, Brodhurst. Continue with the story. Explain what connection the unfortunate episode with that young lady has on your recent escape." Just then Sir Edmund's eyes widened as he hit upon a surprising notion. "Good God! Surely your red-faced, grasping female and that shy young thing are not one and the same?" But as the older man saw the truth of the statement written in his friend's face, he shook his head slowly in disbelief. "Finish your tale, old chap. This whole affair is beyond imagining." He sat down in a high-backed leather chair and crossed his legs, preparing himself for a protracted story.

Brodhurst paced back and forth. "I'm of the same mind, Edmund. You haven't heard the half of it." His nose wrinkled in disgust. "Now we come to the despicable plot which was hatched against me. Two months past, her father contacted me. He arranged a meeting and then related a strange tale of our two families agreeing to a marriage between myself and his daughter at the time of her birth. She and I were not told, however, supposedly to give ample time for a natural affinity to develop, once she had made her debut. When my father left this world unexpectedly without telling me of these plans, the lady's parent waited for the customary mourning period to end before approaching me, or so he stated. He failed, however, to inform me his daughter has withdrawn from social contact due to a vile and deforming affliction."

He filled both glasses from the decanter and handed one to Edmund before taking a sip of his own and continuing. "The story seemed odd, I admit, but it seemed possible there was a grain of truth in it. My mother had already left for her tour of the Continent, so I was unable to consult her. In any event, the father assured me—completely falsely— that the lady in question had matured into a lovely creature. He also assured me that her inheritance was considerable."

Edmund interrupted his friend's narration. "Hang it all, Jonathan, money has never been important to you before this. In addition, my friend, there are a hundred pretty faces on damsels of suitable background who are most anxious and willing to be your bride. Surely that piece about an agreement between your families was a Banbury tale. You didn't seriously believe it, did you?"

Brodhurst turned and stared out the window again, seeing only gray shapes in the misty twilight. "No, I didn't swallow the story in its entirety. But as I said, our families had been acquainted at one time, though in recent years there had been no contact. I imagined there had been some talk between fond mamas. I did feel that this was their way of informing me the lady finally acknowledged her error of indifference toward me, and that she was no longer aloof, but rather interested. In truth, I admit to being flattered that she would go to such lengths to gain my attention."

He paused momentarily, his eyes clouded in deep thought. He couldn't bring himself to reveal, even to his friend, the rush of elation he had felt when the earl had opened the way for him to renew his acquaintance with the girl who had affected him so strangely. He remembered how he had wanted to jump at the chance to make amends for his churlish behavior toward her in London.

Sir Edmund broke into his friend's reverie. "Go on, go on. Don't leave me hanging like this. So you were flattered. What then?"

Jonathan finished his glass, using the time to compose himself. "Naturally, I gave the matter considerable thought. After all, now that I have inherited, marriage is essential if the line is to be secured. The lady's background is impeccable, and of course, after the losses my father suffered, an infusion of fresh capital would certainly expedite my plans for modernizing the farms. I expected to have a marchioness of unexceptionable breeding and looks, and an heiress as well. All told, the situation seemed quite acceptable, so I agreed and the bargain was struck. All that was left was for me to call upon the lady and offer for her formally."

Brodhurst hesitated; his jaw tightened and his hand clenched into a fist as he remembered the morning's events. Although he hated to admit it, his sense of betrayal had been made far more bitter because he had embarked with a secret hope of having found a perfect mate. Taking a deep breath, he began to relate what he had encountered at Wynford Manor.

"Thank God I made an unexpected visit," he commented after describing what he had seen. "I would not have known had I preceded my visit with a note of warning. They can put on a proper face when the occasion warrants, I'm sure. But I'll wager the fortune is all a hum, conceived for the express purpose of helping her to snare a husband. No heiress ever dons clothes such as she wore this morning unless forced to by the most dire circumstances. It's certain I was not meant to see her in such a state. Although I swear I'll never know how they planned to hide her features."

He stroked his forehead for a moment as he remembered the intensity of his disappointment when first he suspected her deceitfulness. The pain had been so deep and unexpected that in defense he had turned it into anger and directed it toward the source of the problem, namely the lady Alicia herself. The extent of his rage had surprised even him, and he had realized his scathing rebuke had stung her cruelly. But she had brought it all on herself and had deserved every word, he reminded himself, thereby banishing the faint feeling of guilt which had begun to appear.

"Well, to finish the story, this morning brought an end to the entire affair," the marquess said. "I saw through their little scheme and escaped in time. The Earl of Wynford and his daughter must turn to some other poor chap for their financial salvation. I certainly pity the man."

Sir Edmund produced a small handkerchief and wiped his forehead thoughtfully. "Wynford, did you say? He's a right one, I'll be bound. Rich as Croesus, too. He simply couldn't be the slyboots you described. There must be some mistake."

"No mistake," Brodhurst replied. "Either the earl has had an extreme financial setback and his pockets are to let, or he is by far the most cheese-paring tightfist I have ever met. I cannot conceive of a man treating his only child in such a shabby manner. No, they simply must have come down in the world. That seems to be the only possible rationale for such a scene as I witnessed this morning."

Edmund shook his head in disbelief. "The earl may have had certain financial reversals, but I can't believe his basic nature has changed so drastically. I met him a few years back. He seemed a fine, honest, straightforward type, one you could count on in a tight squeeze. The way he took care of his half-sister, Lady Matilda, is a case in point. He did a fine job, especially since there was such a difference in their ages. He certainly saw to it that she married well. It's beyond belief that he turned to such deceitful ways. Shameful, if it's true."

Brodhurst shook his head. "The picture you paint certainly isn't the one I've been privy to see. I own my first impression was much like yours, but the earl's subsequent actions belie that. Why he was absolutely adamant about his daughter receiving a generous allowance. Come to think of it, he actually had the figure written into our agreement."

At that moment the marquess froze, his face slowly turning a deep red—due in part to embarrassment as well as anger—as he remembered the legal document. "That damnable piece of paper!" he exclaimed. "It completely slipped my mind!"

"Surely you didn't sign anything?" Edmund questioned, deeply concerned.

"By God, I did," the marquess acknowledged, pounding his forehead with his fist. "Idiot that I am, I signed a nuptial agreement."

Sir Edmund pursed his lips in thought for a moment before remarking, "Since the earl seems to have been less than truthful about his finances, certainly the contract can be nullified."

Brodhurst hurried to the desk and frantically searched until he found the offensive document. He scrutinized it carefully, then looked up slowly.

"Damme, Edmund, I've got myself in quite a mess!" He slammed the paper down. "There's nothing stated about his actual financial situation, merely that the Lady Alicia is his sole heiress, and will receive everything. By God! He was probably referring to his debts, not his assets!"

"Is there no way, then, to break the contract?" Sir Edmund asked, his voice full of worry.

"Oh, yes, most certainly," Jonathan replied cynically. "Lady Alicia has the right to withdraw at any time. No reason need be given." He slowly began to smile, relief showing in his eyes. "Naturally, after my unforgivable rudeness, no lady could possibly continue to consider me suitable for marriage."

"Unless, of course, her needs are so pressing as to outweigh all the disadvantages," Sir Edmund shrewdly interjected.

"Let us sincerely hope that such is not the case," Brodhurst replied, "or perhaps I can buy my way out."

Alicia peered closely at her image in the mirror and examined her face thoroughly. The sunburn had completely healed, although all the skin had peeled off first. That period had been painful and unsightly, but the results, were quite pleasing to the young lady, and she smiled thankfully as she rose to finish dressing.

"Oh, my lady, you've a complexion that's even prettier than before, and that's a fact," Mary said as she helped her mistress into a dove gray carriage dress. "It's as fine and fresh as a newborn's, all pink and glowing."

Alicia stood quietly gazing into the mirror as Mary's nimble fingers worked quickly to button her up the back. "Yes, Mary, but unfortunately it seems a trifle too pink, don't you think?"

A voice from the doorway broke into their conversation. "Don't worry yourself on that head, my dear," Lady Matilda instructed, then entered the bedroom in the manner of a captain taking charge of his ship. "It will fade within a week, two at the very most I should think. In any event, it will be quite an acceptable color by the time we start parading before the ton, have no fear." She looked at the young maid who was still fussing about the table. "Now, Mary, hurry downstairs. James and Edward are coming to carry down the luggage, and you should be ready to leave."

Mary curtsied quickly. "Yes, m'lady. I've but to fetch my cloak and bonnet, and I'm ready to go." With a titter of excitement she hurried out of the room.

Matilda turned her attention to the room, perusing the baggage (trunks, portmanteaus, and boxes of all shapes and sizes) which was scattered around. "Oh, it is sincerely to be hoped that she hasn't packed *all* your belongings for our few months in London. Sometimes I think she has more hair than wit, and that applies to her mistress as well." She softened this reproach with laughing eyes and a quick smile.

Alicia gave a mock frown before forcing a bright smile. She knew how carefully her aunt had planned their re-entry into Society. "Please don't fret. Your instructions have been followed as closely as possible. Mary and I packed only what we felt was absolutely essential. Most of these pieces of luggage are empty as you requested."

Matilda nodded approvingly, obviously pleased with the extent to which her plans were progressing. "Good, good! There will be plenty of silks and laces with which to fill them once we have visited the shops in Bond Street. Your dresses are fine enough for the country, but in London, you must wear nothing that is not the very height of fashion. And so, when we return to Wynford Manor for the summer, you may well need all this baggage and more to accommodate your new fineries." She stopped for a moment, her eyes glowing with excitement. "I own the mere thought of shopping is enough to make my heart race. Oh, my dear, I must confess I am anticipating the gaiety of London with more than a modicum of pleasure."

Alicia's large blue eyes sparkled also, but there was more anxiety than excitement involved. She hesitated to tell her aunt of the swarm of butterflies which seemed to invade her stomach every time the trip was mentioned, hoping to keep from spoiling Matilda's pleasure. Her aunt seemed to have forgotten the real reason for going to London.

Matilda took her niece's hand, squeezing it reassuringly. "Stop your worrying, child. It will all come about in a fine manner, I'm sure. What happened when you were seventeen is all past and forgotten. Your circumstances will be greatly improved this time around. Goodness! Whatever could your father and I have been thinking of when we let you have your first Season before your eighteenth birthday?" She shook her head slowly in bewilderment of their past actions. "You certainly were not ready for such an experience, and to have you introduced by your godmother, Lady Sanderson, was folly in the extreme. My, what a pair of muddleheads we were."

"It wasn't that bad, Aunt Matilda. And what happened was most assuredly not your fault," Alicia reassured her.

"Well, whose fault was it then, if not mine? Certainly it was not yours, child. I was too ill at the time to accompany you myself, and your father wanted you off to London as soon as possible to fix your interest on your future husband, or so he hoped. Anyway, I suggested Lady Sanderson, and it was all a disaster of the worst sort."

She stopped for a moment to catch her breath, then bent and gave her niece a tiny kiss on a glowing cheek. "It will be much more enjoyable for you this time, dear. Rest assured on that count. You are going to be the rage of all London, mark my words. Now, I daresay I have been rambling on much too much. There's still a great deal that must be seen to before our departure."

She sailed out of the room just as James and Edward, the two footmen, presented themselves at the door. They made short work of clearing the bedroom of all trunks and boxes.

Before Alicia left, she studied her reflection carefully, finally nodding in satisfaction at her appearance. The warm carriage dress was trimmed with maroon frogging down the front in military style. Braiding of the same color circled the waist and traced all the seams of the skirt. Her matching gray bonnet, with a wide brim, was also trimmed in that particular shade of dark red, and the silk sash was tied under her ear in a saucy bow.

Alicia refrained from letting down the heavy veil attached to the brim. It hid her face completely, protecting the delicate skin from the sun's harmful rays. But it also made walking difficult, since the veil nearly had the same effect as a blindfold in the dimness of the house's interior. It was best left up until the moment of departure. She wasn't going to expose her face even for the moment it took to climb into the carriage.

As Alicia descended the stairs, she heard the coach carrying Mary, Matilda's maid, and the luggage moving slowly along the driveway toward the road. It would arrive at the house in town before she and her aunt did, or so it was to be hoped. They were leaving later, but their traveling carriage was lighter and faster than the one used by the servants.

The earl and his sister were waiting in the small but cheerful breakfast room, enjoying tea and toast. Alicia joined them, but accepted only some tea preferring to travel on an empty stomach.

Spirited conversation was decidedly lacking in the small group, and the only discussion, if one could call it that, was confined to the weather and condition of the roads. Mostly, the three sat quietly, each immersed in his or her own thoughts.

Alicia knew her father loved her and his sister dearly and wanted only their happiness. But he also gained much pleasure and comfort from their presence. She was aware he did not anticipate with pleasure a solitary life in the large manor. In fact, she suspected he was having a difficult time keeping from appearing downright glum. She herself knew the feeling well and took a deep breath, trying to banish the wisps of depression which seemed to be settling around her.

Trent, the butler, broke up the quiet little gathering when he announced that the carriage was waiting. He led the procession down the hall. The staff had lined up by the door to say goodbye and wish them well. When she saw the cook, Alicia approached her to once again express appreciation for the amazing salve which had worked its wonders on her sunburn. When the ladies finally passed through the door, the cook stood tall, a large smile of pride on her face and a small tear in her eye which she quickly wiped away with her apron.

The earl kissed them gently on the forehead, holding his daughter a trifle longer than was necessary, then helped them up into the carriage. "Be careful, my dears, but most important, be happy." He stepped back, gave Coombs, the coachman, the sign to leave, and turned back to the house, not willing to watch his loved ones depart.

Coombs flipped the ribbons gently, and the horses started off smartly, the carriage swaying gently as it traveled down the drive. Thomas rode Starfire and followed closely behind the coach as he led the gentle gray gelding which was Lady Matilda's mount.

The carriage soon turned onto the post road and headed south toward London. Alicia stared out at the passing countryside. Rolling hills, stands of trees, open fields separated by rows of hedges, all were covered in that lovely spring green that spoke silently of rebirth and the promise of a full and luxuriant summer.

A new beginning, she mused, in her life as well as the land. Without conscious effort on her part, Alicia's tension slowly faded as the journey progressed, and she began to enjoy herself.

Her aunt was also staring out the window, and Alicia wondered if she were planning their strategy once they arrived in London, or if she were merely enjoying the scenery. Whichever the case might be, Alicia refrained from breaking their mutual silence. She was thankful that her aunt was not one of those ladies whose incessant prattle acted as a continual source of irritation to the nerves and mental processes of all those unfortunates who found themselves in close proximity. Lady Matilda could carry on a spirited conversation when called upon to do so, but she also enjoyed silent companionship.

Near noon, Coombs pulled the carriage to a halt at a small inn so that the horses could be changed. After obtaining a private room, the ladies sat down to enjoy a small luncheon, Cook having furnished the carriage with a large basket of food for their journey. Cups of tea were ordered, and they opened the basket to find cold sliced chicken, biscuits, cheese, and the last of the spiced apple rings that Cook had put up last fall. The amount of food was much too great for two such diminutive ladies, so they sent the basket down to Thomas and Coombs, who were pleased to make short work of consuming its contents entirely.

Thoroughly refreshed, the quartet resumed their journey south. Both Alicia and her aunt succumbed to the rocking motion of the carriage and dozed off, allowing the miles to pass unnoticed. When they did waken, it was to a gray and chilly greeting. The sun, which had been so bright early that morning, was now hidden by a thick blanket of clouds. The wind had picked up, and the temperature had dropped sharply.

Alicia raised her veil, since the sun was no longer a threat, and looked at the clouds, her expressive eyes filled with worry. "I hope it won't rain so hard as to hinder our progress."

"It certainly could become most unpleasant," Matilda said as she placed her hand outside and found it quickly covered by tiny drops of water. "The rain has already begun."

What had started as a fine sprinkle soon became a steady rain. Ruts quickly filled with water, and the roadway became quite treacherous.

A phaeton, whose driver was anxious to reach his destination before being soaked to the skin, came up behind them at a speed greater than was safe for the prevailing conditions, and made to pass. Coombs pulled over as far as possible to give the impatient gentleman plenty of room. Unfortunately he could not judge the depth of the water-covered wheel marks on the side of the road. The front wheel dropped into a deep rut. The carriage tilted ominously, and the spokes were forced against a stone which jutted out from the side of the trough. There was a sharp crack, and the conveyance slowly tilted down on its side like a ship sinking in a sea of mud.

Coombs jumped down to steady the horses who, thankfully, were unhurt. The stranger, an extremely youthful gentleman, quickly pulled up his team and hurried to assist him. In the meantime, Thomas had reached the carriage door and opened it to find the two ladies slightly disheveled, but otherwise unharmed. While Coombs surveyed the damage, the young gentleman joined Thomas, and together they easily lifted Lady Matilda out of the carriage. He then reached down to take Alicia's hand, but hesitated when she looked directly up at him, her face pale, and her huge blue eyes dark with fear and worry. Such lovely features nearly paralyzed him as he gazed in simple adoration.

Alicia, slightly vexed at the stranger's inaction, turned to the young groom. "Thomas, do help me out. The gentleman seems to prefer keeping me a prisoner in here."

This sharp comment spurred the young man into action, and he put both hands around the tiny waist to lift her out of the carriage. She was small and light, and his expression seemed to imply that he thought her an angel, able to float down on invisible wings.

Coombs interrupted this charming tableau with distressing news. "I be truly sorry to tell her ladyship, but the wheel's broke, good and proper. There'll be no more traveling this day, leastways not 'til it's fixed."

"Oh dear, things are in a sorry state," Alicia remarked, "but we can't just stand here talking about our condition. I don't look forward to a bout with pneumonia which will surely come if shelter isn't found soon."

Her call for something to be done was all the stranger needed to set him in motion. He offered his arms to both Alicia and her aunt. "Ladies, allow me to escort you to my phaeton. Although not completely enclosed, it will offer you some semblance of shelter until we reach Milton, which is only a short distance ahead. The town boasts of quite a respectable inn, the Lance and Shield. I myself was making for that very hostlery when misfortune overtook your Brougham." He spoke as he walked, helping the ladies across the muddy roadway and up into his phaeton.

Thomas strapped two of the ladies' smaller bags on the back of the phaeton, then brought the carriage rugs from the Brougham. Soon the ladies were bundled warmly as they huddled in cramped quarters, three on a perch meant to hold only two. They started off briskly, leaving Thomas and Coombs to unharness the horses and follow on foot.

Before springing the horses, the young gentleman spoke. "Perhaps we should take this moment for introductions." Tipping his hat with a flair unusual in so youthful a gentleman, he announced himself, "Geoffrey Baugh at your service, ladies."

"Baugh?" Lady Matilda repeated. "Isn't that the family name of the Earl of Selcester?"

He nodded and grinned. "I am the youngest of the earl's six sons. I am on my way to London to visit a relative." He glanced quickly at Alicia, then turned his attention back to the horses before continuing. "Perhaps I might experience some of the life known to be found only in that most exciting city."

Lady Matilda appeared to approve, for she introduced Alicia and herself. Alicia lowered her head in lieu of a curtsy, which was of course impossible under the circumstances. She eyed Mr. Baugh under lowered lashes and noted that he looked quite dashing in his three-caped driving coat and top hat of beaver. He handled the ribbons adequately, although she would have preferred a slower pace, even if it meant remaining in the rain for a longer time. The phaeton was light, built for speed and cornering, and it seemed rather insubstantial. Since she felt her seat was precarious enough as it was, she was heartily grateful that the gentleman did not drive a high-perch which she had heard was quite the rage with the younger set.

Matilda continued the conversation. "Perhaps we shall meet under better circumstances, for we, too, are on our way to London to enjoy the Season.

"I see lights ahead," Alicia interrupted. "It is to be hoped our destination is near." She peered through the rain and waning light and was rewarded with the sight of a large building with stables at its rear. They pulled in under a faded sign of a knight's lance and shield.

Geoffrey Baugh helped his passengers down and escorted them into the inn. He bespoke rooms for them all, made certain the luggage would be brought up, then took his leave to oversee the care of the horses.

A maid led Alicia and her aunt to their rooms and helped them out of their wet clothing. Before long they were comfortably sipping tea and discussing the events of the day. A small sneeze from Alicia, however, brought a quick end to their conversation. An alarmed Matilda immediately ordered the young girl to bed for a rest before dinner.

With only a mild protest, Alicia acquiesced to her aunt's demand and was soon enjoying the delicious warmth created as she snuggled under a heavy comforter. She fell asleep almost immediately.

She slept into the evening and, feeling much refreshed, was up and dressed when a small knock announced her aunt. Matilda was followed by a maid carrying a tray of steaming soup and fresh bread, which she placed on the table. Matilda dismissed the maid and came to stand by Alicia's bed.

"I did not waken you for dinner, my dear, for fear that your sneeze was but the precursor of a much more serious condition, in which case you needed rest more than sustenance."

"I feel perfectly fine now," Alicia responded and sat down to enjoy her meal.

Matilda continued chatting. "I just returned from speaking with young Mr. Baugh. He informed me that a wheelwright has been summoned, and repairs should be completed by midmorning tomorrow. Such a charming gentleman, you know, and I could tell you have made a conquest there by the look of dejection on his face when I explained that you would not be joining us."

"Oh, fustian! We only just met." Alicia replied. She pretended disinterest, but a little smile betrayed her pleasure at catching the eye of such a handsome and dashing young gentleman. "I seriously doubt that we shall meet again," she continued. "Most likely Mr. Baugh will spend his time at White's, not at Almack's."

"I seriously doubt that, my dear, and so would you if you had the benefit of the information I received this evening."

Her words sparked Alicia's interest. "I own it would be quite comforting to find him present at some of those dull soirees we shall be obliged to attend once we arrive in London." She sighed, then smiled sweetly and returned to her soup.

Matilda leaned forward as if to impart a great secret. "It was not my intention to speak of this to you, my dear, in the hope of surprising you later. But I simply cannot hold it longer." She hesitated for a moment before continuing, enjoying the teasing silence and the look of expectancy on her niece's face. Mr. Baugh will be staying with his distant cousin, Lady Sanderson." Upon this pronouncement she sat back to enjoy the effect of her words.

"My godmother?" Alicia asked, astonished.

"The very same," her aunt replied. "Therefore, I am persuaded that our paths shall cross."

"How very interesting," Alicia murmured. She was pleased with the news and smiled as she contemplated their future meeting.

Matilda interrupted her niece's reverie. "There is one other bit of information of which you should be made aware. It is the point upon which I base my certainty that we shall meet the young man again."

"Oh, and what is that?" Alicia asked, perplexed.

"Very simple, my dear, he asked for permission to call upon us at our earliest convenience. And of course I granted it."

# = 4 =

THE LADIES ARRIVED AT their London residence in Cavendish Square on the evening of the following day. It had taken longer to fix the wheel than was first thought, and a late start had been followed by more difficulties and delays due to the poor condition of the roads. Weary from their journey, they partook only lightly of a cold collation and then sought their respective bedrooms for a much needed rest.

Morning found Alicia much refreshed. Accustomed as she was to country hours, she awoke to the sounds of the city with enthusiasm rather than lethargy. Hawkers and fishmongers, carts and barrows—the streets were alive with their activity. Sounds mingled with exotic smells, reminding her that she had eaten very little the night before and was now ravenous.

Mary entered at that moment bearing hot chocolate. "Good morning, m'lady."

Alicia stretched out an eager hand for the cup of chocolate. "Thank you, Mary. I must confess to being famished!"

As her maid left, she began to drink the delicious hot liquid, refusing to allow the proposed activities of the day to interfere with her enjoyment of the morning. Soon Mary returned, followed by a chambermaid bearing a basin of hot water. Alicia finished her toilette in a relaxed manner, finally slipping into a blue dimity morning dress and slippers to match. Her hair was pulled back and pinned in a knot at the nape of her neck. She gave but a cursory glance at her image before leaving the room and going downstairs.

Matilda was pouring tea as Alicia entered the breakfast room. Upon spying her niece, she automatically filled a second cup. "How nice that you could join me, my dear. I was hoping that you would rise early, for we have a great deal to accomplish today."

The young lady helped herself to eggs and kidneys from the sideboard, then sat across from her aunt and began to enjoy her meal.

"What do you have planned?" she asked politely between bites. "I own it would be pleasant to start the day with a lovely ride in the park."

"A ride in the park?" Matilda pursed her lips in disapproval. "Quite out of the question when one considers the other matters which must be attended to in such a short space of time. Riding is perhaps the last activity to be added to our agenda, and probably won't be accomplished for at least a week, if not longer."

Matilda noticed her niece's appearance. "Most assuredly you must not be seen publicly until you are dressed in style; that is the most pressing of our needs at the moment." Her critical eye surveyed Alicia's plain frock and mature hairstyle. "And something must be done about your hair, my dear. That style is much too severe for your lovely features." She hesitated a moment, searching her mind for an appropriate arrangement, then sighed lightly. "Oh dear, I fear I'm just not up on the latest hair fashions. Perhaps, when I see Lady Castlereagh and obtain our vouchers for Almack's, she will recommend a top hairdresser, for I am persuaded your locks need a light touch of the scissors."

At the word scissors, Alicia envisioned all her lovely long hair lying about her on the floor. "Oh no, Aunt Matilda, do not say I must wear it short, for I simply could not bear to have it all cut off!"

Matilda quickly moved to calm her niece's fears. "No, dear, I would never force you into a style you simply could not abide. Now let us leave off worry about hair until a proper dresser is found. Then we can discuss the styles to your satisfaction. At the moment I am persuaded that clothes should be our only concern. Finish your meal now. We mustn't dawdle."

Alicia was informed that the modiste they were to visit was very exclusive, designing only for those whose figure and carriage could display her gowns to their best advantage. Lady Matilda had been one of those fortunates who could wear the lovely dresses, and had become friends with the French designer. Alicia allowed herself to be hurried through breakfast, and soon forgot about haircuts as she discussed silks, laces, colors, and fashions with her aunt. In a much shorter time than one would have expected, she was donning her pelisse and bonnet and joining Lady Matilda in their carriage.

The sun was bright, its warmth reminding Alicia to lower her protective veil before Matilda could admonish her for neglecting something so important. The horses started off briskly, and soon the ladies were deposited in front of a small but fashionable shop on Bond Street. Tiny lettering on the door revealed the proprietor, Madame Bertine. There was no other sign to distinguish it from the many other shops on the busy street, but when Alicia entered and raised her veil, she was aware of thick carpeting which cushioned her feet, cream draperies, and spindle-legged chairs of white and gold which were placed advantageously around the room. A number of mirrors seemed to enlarge the room and accent its simple decor. The entire effect was one of elegance and quality which had been absent in the shops Alicia had visited with her godmother, Lady Sanderson, on her previous stay in London.

Madame Bertine was a petite woman with short black hair generously sprinkled with gray. She was older than Matilda by almost ten years, but her smile upon seeing the lady transformed her face, hiding her age behind dimples and twinkling eyes. Her greeting was effusive, many years having passed since they last met. She welcomed them both to her humble establishment in perfect English, but with an accent decidedly French in origin.

"Your daughter, no?" the modiste questioned as she looked toward Alicia inquiringly.

"Oh my goodness, no." Lady Matilda responded quickly, the smile on her face even broader than before. "Although I am persuaded it would be most pleasant to have her as my very own child, for she is as dear to me as any daughter could possibly be. This is my niece, Lady Alicia, daughter of the Earl of Wynford. I've brought her here to see if she could wear your creations." She turned to her niece before speaking again. "Dear, this is Madame Bertine, whom I consider to be one of the top modistes of all London."

Madame curtsied her acknowledgment of the compliment as well as the introduction, then eyed Alicia critically, walking around to view all angles. Then she requested the young lady to walk back and forth to determine her posture and bearing. After a few minutes of close scrutiny of Alicia's tiny waist, full bosom, fine shoulders, and long graceful neck, she pronounced the young lady quite adequate for her creations.

Matilda was also judged and found to be still worthy of Madame Bertine's gowns, a fact which brought relief to both the aunt and her niece, since any other verdict would have cast Lady Matilda into a fit of the dismals from which she could not have risen for at least a week, if not longer.

Both ladies were quickly ushered to a private fitting room for the countless measurements deemed necessary for obtaining proper fit in the custom-made gowns. To Alicia, they spent what seemed like hours trying on fashions and discussing fabrics and designs.

At last the order was decided upon, and Madame glowed with happy appreciation. Both ladies required complete wardrobes, including walking dresses, morning frocks, riding habits, and gowns for both formal and informal affairs. Heelless slippers in matching materials were also ordered, as well as linen undergarments, exquisitely embroidered by one of the many seamstresses employed by the modiste.

They left the small shop, smiling and exchanging final pleasantries with its proprietor. Alicia was just lowering her lace veil when she caught sight of a splendid pair of matched blacks stepping smartly down Bond Street pulling a bright yellow high-perch phaeton. The traffic was heavy enough to keep the driver busy with the ribbons, and he was thus unable to acknowledge all the smiles, lowering of heads, and tipping of hats which were directed toward him.

Alicia gasped and quickly turned back toward the shop in an attempt to avoid being seen. Matilda looked up to determine what had alarmed her niece, and immediately recognized the driver of the phaeton. "So, Lord Brodhurst is in town," she commented more to herself than to her niece. "Good. Very good."

She turned to Alicia, who by that time had recovered her equanimity, and spoke to her reassuringly. "He didn't see you, dear. Even if he had, it wouldn't signify, for you can't be recognized behind that thick veil." She guided Alicia gently down the walk, chatting pleasantly to cover the embarrassing moment. "There's our carriage now. Oh dear, I fear Coombs will be in quite a fret, for we are much later than I had planned. Unlike men, horses should never be kept waiting, you know."

The second footman jumped down to assist them into the barouche, and soon the ladies were settled comfortably and on their way back to Cavendish Square. Alicia's knees were still a trifle weak, and she was relieved to sit after the unsettling appearance of the marquess. She knew it was inevitable that they would meet, but she had been unprepared for the sight of him looking so dashing and unconcerned as he drove down the street. She remembered their last meeting, recalling the look of disgust in his eyes. He once had the power to make her weak and breathless, to render her speechless, but she despised him now. This time she had a certain amount of power over him, she knew, and by the time they reached their house on Cavendish Square, she was feeling quite pleased about the entire situation.

That afternoon found the ladies in the small drawing room. Alicia was embroidering and Matilda was poring over a list of friends she planned to invite to their first dinner party when Babcock announced Mr. Moffitt, the earl's man of business.

Mr. Moffitt was a pleasant man of middle age. He graciously asked after the ladies' health, and was visibly overset when informed of the problems which beset their journey to London.

His purpose in calling upon the ladies was to ascertain their comfort and degree of satisfaction with the house and its servants. Also he wondered if his services were required in any other matters. The ladies were quick to voice their pleasure with the surroundings, although Lady Matilda did express some disappointment in the decor of the dining room as well as the large drawing room, which was sadly outmoded.

"I hope, my lady, that the rooms can quickly be changed to your satisfaction. His Lordship has made such ample funds available for the housekeeping that you may order such furnishings as you desire." Mr. Moffitt's eyes gleamed with pride at the generosity and consideration of his employer. "I hope that everything else is to your ladyship's satisfaction."

"Of course," Alicia said. "Mr. Moffitt, it appears you have chosen an exemplary staff. The cook is excellent."

"Babcock informs me he worked for Lady Twillaby, who is, as we all know, a most notable hostess," Lady Matilda said. "I collect we are extremely fortunate to have been able to engage him. I wonder, Mr. Moffitt, what inducement you used to entice him to our establishment?"

Mr. Moffitt, pleased that his efforts on behalf of the ladies were being recognized, but slightly embarrassed by their praise, informed them that Lord and Lady Twillaby had gone abroad for a year and had closed their London house. Matilda thanked Mr. Moffitt graciously and was about to bring the interview to an end when she remembered one other matter in which he could be of service. A dancing master was needed for Lady Alicia so that she could polish her steps and eliminate any awkwardness she might retain after having absented herself from London balls for such a long time.

Mr. Moffitt understood the confidentiality of the mission, realizing the embarrassment a young lady might endure if it were known she required dancing lessons at such an advanced age. He assured both ladies that everything would be handled quite tactfully, and they could expect to interview a suitable instructor within a day, two at the most.

Alicia liked the man and smiled warmly as he took his leave of them. Babcock showed him to the door, then returned to the drawing room to inform the ladies that a letter had been left while they were closeted with Mr. Moffitt.

"Who is it from?" Alicia queried excitedly.

Matilda opened the letter and a knowing smile appeared on her face. Without a word she handed it to her niece who quickly read the few words addressed to Lady Matilda, but inquiring after the health of both ladies.

"Your obedient servant, Geoffrey Baugh," Alicia read aloud. "I don't believe it!" Her eyes were wide with incredulity as she spoke.

"I remember mentioning that he had asked permission to call upon us," Matilda reminded her niece. "But I must confess to being not a little astonished at his taking the trouble to write. One must own that it is a trifle flattering, don't you agree?"

Alicia nodded, coloring with pleasure at the idea Mr. Baugh was paying her particular attention. The thought that she was able to attract the interest of such a handsome gentleman did wonders for her self-confidence.

The next few days passed quickly for Alicia as she immersed herself completely in the preparations for her reentry into the social world. Mornings were devoted to fittings at Madame Bertine's and shopping for accessories to complete her wardrobe. At the milliner's, she ordered smart and dashing bonnets, made in such a way that the heavy veiling she required appeared an attractive trimming when lifted over the brim and draped against the crown.

Afternoons were partially filled with dance lessons. The instructor Mr. Moffitt had sent to them was a slightly built gentleman of medium height, a pleasant smile, and polished manners. His soft voice and retiring nature pleased Alicia immensely, since she remembered her first dancing master as being a loud-voiced tyrant.

The instructor seemed unduly interested in teaching the intricate steps of many little-known country dances, but Alicia was able to keep him occupied trying to refresh her memory of the more popular dances of the day. The cotillion required a great deal of concentration, since it consisted of many complicated figures and allowed almost an endless variety of steps. In the dance, one couple would lead, requiring the remaining dancers to follow their steps and patterns, thus making it necessary for Alicia to know all the figures before attempting the dance in public.

The quadrille was enjoyable, but Alicia's favorite dance was the waltz, which of course the dancing master considered quite shocking. Lady Matilda was of the opinion that it was fast becoming the rage and quite appropriate for a young lady past her first Season. She overrode all objections, and the dance was included in the lessons.

Lady Matilda enjoyed watching her niece, who appeared to become more graceful and self-assured with each lesson, and even practiced a few steps herself, so that no one would notice even the slightest bit of awkwardness on her part after a ten-year absence from London.

After the dancing lesson was completed, the ladies always settled themselves in the small parlor for a comfortable coze. Alicia listened to her aunt relate stories of the eccentricities of certain of the more noted hostesses she would meet in the next few weeks. With each new story, Alicia lost more of her awe of these magnificent leaders of the haute ton and began to think of them as interesting and unusual ladies whom she would enjoy meeting. In this gentle manner, Alicia was led by her aunt into a new attitude about the ton, one in which she could consider herself just as deserving of recognition and acceptance as anyone.

On the afternoon of her tenth day in London, Alicia sat in the drawing room composing a short missive to her father. Her aunt sat nearby, embroidering a delicate tracery of rosebuds on a small square of fine linen. Both ladies were relaxed, happy to have some quiet moments after the hectic preparations of the past few days. The dancing lessons had at last been concluded, the new gowns all completed, and the last of the new furniture delivered to their house. Invitations to Lady Matilda's oldest friends had been sent out for a dinner two weeks hence. They were enjoying the calm of this early afternoon knowing there would soon be chaotic activity which accompanies full acceptance by the ton.

Babcock's sonorous voice startled the ladies as he announced the presence of Lady Sanderson and Mr. Baugh. Lady Sanderson, wearing a purple sarsenet round gown and matching turban, rushed into the room, her young companion following somewhat hesitantly. She gave Matilda a perfunctory greeting, and turned quickly to embrace her astonished goddaughter.

"Oh, my dear child, I must say it was such an agreeable surprise when Geoffrey apprised me of your arrival. How horrible it must have been for you to have such an accident on your journey down here, although I own I'm always fearful that such things might happen when I'm forced to make any journey myself, the roads being what they are these days, but of course you had no way of knowing, for I'm sure it's been simply years since you've traveled them."

Lady Sanderson stopped to catch her breath, then cast a reassuring smile upon her companion, who stood discreetly behind and slightly to her right. With a small motion of her hand, she brought him forward to face her goddaughter, then, in the high-pitched voice Alicia remembered so well, continued speaking. "How fortunate for you that dear Geoffrey was near to help, which I'm persuaded was quite providential, for he was expected to arrive in London the previous day, but was delayed due to problems of his own, which I've yet to completely understand, and so was near to be of service in your hour of need, for which we must all be extremely grateful."

Alicia turned to her second guest, her face alight with a broad smile of welcome mixed with one of amusement. She fought the uncharitable urge to inform the woman that it was Mr. Baugh's haste which had precipitated the problem, realizing it would only embarrass the gentleman. Instead, she turned mirth-filled eyes up to him. "Yes, I'm most grateful for the service you rendered to us, Mr. Baugh, and I am pleased to have the opportunity to express my gratitude in person. You left the inn much too early the following morning for me to do so at that time."

The young gentleman shook himself out of the incipient paralysis which had seized him the very moment Alicia turned her huge blue eyes in his direction. He took the hand she proffered, bowed low, and kissed it in a magnificent fashion. "Please say no more, my lady. I am the person who should be expressing gratitude. I was greatly honored to have the opportunity to serve such charm and beauty as yours." As he spoke he was disconcerted to see a slight frown pass across the young lady's face. Then, remembering his words, he was pleased to see her face relax as he finished his sentence properly. "And your aunt's, of course."

Alicia smiled her approval and was prepared to continue the conversation, when Lady Matilda summoned Geoffrey to her side. "Come sit here, Mr. Baugh," she said, patting the space beside her on the sofa. "I too wish to express my gratitude, not only for your kind assistance after our mishap but also for the thoughtfulness which brought you to our door to ascertain if we had arrived safely."

The young man appeared somewhat flustered by Lady Matilda's praise, but reluctantly excused himself from Alicia and sat down next to her aunt. His eyes, however, strayed often, coming to rest on the young lady he had just left. Lady Sanderson had already brought a chair close and was prepared for a comfortable coze with her goddaughter.

"Tell me, my dear, what prompted this visit to London, for I completely left off hoping to see you return after you missed your second Season, which was a very boring one, I might add, and was quite deserving of being missed." She shook her head sadly, remembering the scarcity of scandals that year, then continued, broaching the subject which plainly was the main reason for her visit.

"Dear child, I've heard nothing in the past two years concerning an engagement between you and some eligible gentleman; therefore, I feel that I may have been somewhat remiss not to have urged you sooner to start an earnest search for a suitable husband, although I am reminded of your father's words to me some time ago when he said that he had arranged for things to come about in their proper time. Have you perhaps arrived in London to procure a trousseau? Can we expect an announcement in the *Times*?"

The deep blush which rose to Alicia's cheeks at these words brought a gleam of triumph to Lady Sanderson's eyes, but it quickly faded with the young lady's denial.

"No, no, you are mistaken. I am not engaged," Alicia responded quickly, noting that the question had come much nearer the truth than she was pleased to admit. She knew that her godmother was a good-hearted woman, but slightly scatterbrained, and unable to keep a secret for more than a day. So Alicia's words were designed to allay suspicions that her visit was connected in any respect with an engagement.

"I must confess it was Aunt Matilda who finally convinced me to return and enjoy some of the gaiety of city life before committing myself completely to a rustic existence in the country," Alicia said cheerfully. "But we are here to enjoy the rest of the Season, not to seek a husband," she added, responding to Lady Sanderson's earlier words. She spoke with an air of authority, bringing an expression of disappointment to Lady Sanderson's face.

"Well, my dear, I own I could never be so very positive about such an occurrence, for one never knows when one will meet a most eligible gentleman who would suit admirably." She smiled and glanced at the young man chatting with Lady Matilda. "Who knows," she continued thoughtfully, "who knows, indeed." With that enigmatic pronouncement, she began donning her gloves.

Mr. Baugh, made aware that it was time to take his leave, excused himself and approached Alicia. "Many thanks for allowing us to descend upon you this afternoon," he said quietly. "I sadly regret that we had so little time to converse. Perhaps you would receive me again at some later date?" he asked hopefully, his eyes as well as his voice imploring.

"Please feel free to call upon us whenever you are so inclined," Alicia replied warmly. "Your presence would be most welcome."

The young man smiled broadly, and ventured to invite her and Lady Matilda to ride with him some morning of her choosing. Both Alicia and her aunt accepted with enthusiasm, and plans were finalized for the next day. The guests took their leave, both quite content with the results of their visit.

The following morning found Mr. Baugh escorting the ladies in a slow and genteel trot down Rotten Row. Lady Matilda, looking much younger than her years in the smart green habit designed especially for her by Madame Bertine, was trying rather unsuccessfully to keep a lively conversation going. Mr. Baugh was of little help in this endeavor, for he seemed content to ride silently, watching the lady on his right with admiring eyes.

Alicia was attired in a deep blue velvet habit trimmed with powderblue frogging down the front. A smart hat sat atop her head, and to it was attached the heavy veiling which was pulled tightly over her chin and caught up at the crown with a cluster of small velvet bows of the same color as the frogging. Even though her face could hardly be discerned, the effect was still quite charming.

The air was cool and moist, carrying the aroma of damp earth and green plants. Alicia was suddenly intensely homesick for her country life. She longed to snatch the hat and veil from her head, to urge Starfire to a run and feel free, letting the wind whip through her long hair and sting her cheeks. But, of course, in London such an action would stamp her as a hoyden and create some difficulty in trying to gain acceptance in the highest circles of the ton. Nevertheless, she continued to daydream, until a comment from Lady Matilda brought her back to an awareness of her surroundings.

"Alicia, dear, I do believe we are being approached by two gentlemen, one of whom appears to be the Marquess of Brodhurst."

Alicia looked ahead and saw two riders advancing toward them. One was tall and of a proud bearing, unmistakably that of Lord Brodhurst; the other, though not quite so commanding a figure, but just as graceful in the saddle, was a stranger to her.

Matilda leaned over and gently patted her niece's hand. "Courage," she whispered, and then straightened to greet the gentlemen.

Lord Brodhurst, riding with his friend, Sir Edmund Coswell, recognized Lady Matilda and reined in his horse, greeting her civilly. Introductions were made all around, and the group began to move slowly along the path the Marquess had just traveled. Lady Matilda included both Sir Edmund and Mr. Baugh in her conversation, so that Alicia and Lord Brodhurst would quite naturally fall in behind where they could converse privately.

Alicia, holding herself proudly erect and feeling remarkably calm under the circumstances, addressed her escort coolly. "Sir, you honor me beyond all expectations with your presence by my side. I do believe you expressed a desire to avoid any such situation when last we conversed."

"My respects to your ladyship's memory, but I recall no such statement. Perhaps you allude to my expression of distaste in reference to your sharing Brodhurst Manor as my wife." He knew his words were boorish and ill-mannered, but they were designed to discourage the lady from any thoughts of prolonging their relationship.

Unfortunately, his speech served only to strengthen Alicia's resolve to carry through with her plan. "Ah, yes, I confess you have the right of it," she responded pleasantly, as if she had not heard him. Because the veiling hid her face, Brodhurst was unaware of the grim set to her mouth and the cold glint in her eyes. "Such an unfortunate situation, I must say," she continued, "for I admit to having experienced a desire to make that estate my home." She shook her head slowly in an expression of sadness.

"Yes, I can well believe you might," the marquess responded heartily, his expression a mixture of distaste and bafflement. It was plain he had not expected her attitude to be either so pleasant or so forthright.

"Well, no matter," Alicia continued, "I have no doubts I shall manage quite well elsewhere. Have you perhaps some place in mind?" she asked in an agreeable tone.

"Why no," he responded almost automatically, his brows knitted in perplexity. "Where you reside is your decision, of course."

"Why, how very kind you are, sir. I own I would not have thought it of you after our last meeting." She bowed her head slightly as if to acknowledge his thoughtfulness.

"Kindness has nothing to do with it," he quickly retorted, his voice tinged with anger at his inability to discern the direction of her thoughts. "Your activities are none of my concern."

"But sir, I assumed you would be responsible for my conduct," she said demurely.

"I hardly think so," he replied gruffly. "No one could possibly hold me accountable for your actions." He spoke authoritatively, but his uneasiness and sense of foreboding were quite apparent. It even transferred itself to his mount, which began to shy and prance excessively. Lord Brodhurst took a few moments to calm the spirited animal sufficiently to continue the conversation. "I am at a loss to understand how you could consider me responsible for the things you have done."

"Oh, pray forgive me if I have led your thoughts astray, for I had no intention of implying that you should answer for my past actions, only for future ones."

Lord Brodhurst blanched visibly, but his voice betrayed no hint of emotion. "My dear lady, I fear you have been greatly misinformed. I shall not be held accountable for your actions either in the past or the future. Your business is of no concern to me."

"Forgive me for my ignorance, sir," Alicia replied. "My understanding of certain legalities is very poor indeed, and it was very bad of me to disgrace myself so." She hesitated for only a moment and then spoke in her sweetest tone. "I was under the impression that a man was responsible for the affairs of his wife."

She had delivered the thrust with the skill of a duelist, and Brodhurst's eyes widened with understanding as her intent sank in.

"Good God, woman! You don't mean . . . you can't possibly intend . . ." He stopped, squared his shoulders, and spoke more slowly, his voice quivering ever so slightly from his immense effort at emotional control. "Are you implying that we are to be married?"

"Why of course, dear Jonathan. Are we not betrothed?" Her voice seemed to drip honey, but under the veil her eyes reflected the anger and hurt she had suffered.

He winced at her use of his given name, but continued to speak in a measured voice. "Surely you cannot be serious. It's quite obvious we would not suit. Besides, I have not offered for you."

"Oh, that doesn't signify," she replied, waving her tiny hand as if brushing aside all objections. "The agreement has been signed, has it not?" At his slow nod, she continued. "Other than settling upon a date for the ceremony, the matter is quite out of our hands." It was clear her cheerful voice was acting like salt to a wound, for he winced visibly.

"Out of *my* hands, perhaps, but certainly not out of yours, dear lady. It was for the purpose of determining when I might receive your release from that ridiculous contract that I stopped to converse with you this morning. I assumed you would have no objections."

"You are the one who has been misinformed, my lord. I have no intention of releasing you from our nuptial agreement." Her voice, no longer sweet, was cold and cutting, and the set of her shoulders revealed her determination. "I have no more to say on the matter, my lord. We are betrothed!" With those final words, she urged Starfire to a canter and rejoined her aunt and Mr. Baugh. At Alicia's suggestion that it was time to start for home, the three of them took their leave of Sir Edmund.

# = 5 =

LORD BRODHURST JUMPED DOWN from his phaeton and took the steps leading to his house in two bounds. His eyes were clouded and his jaw tightly clenched as he removed his hat and gloves, handing them to his butler without a word. He then strode quickly to the library and entered, slamming the door behind him. The butler and footmen exchanged surprised glances, for such a foul mood was unheard of with his lordship.

Sir Edmund arrived an hour later to find his friend slouched in a deep leather chair, one leg draped over its arm, the other stretched out in front of him. The marquess looked up and acknowledged Sir Edmund's presence with a nod, then returned to staring into the glass of brandy in his hand, a pastime he had been pursuing for some while, between swallows, of course.

"Bad news at the solicitor's?" Edmund asked as he poured himself a drink from the nearly empty decanter. There being no response from his friend, he continued his questioning. "Is there no possible way, then, to break the contract?"

"None whatsoever," Brodhurst replied in a quiet voice, a small sarcastic smile playing at one corner of his mouth. "It seems that felicitations are in order, my friend. I am to be married."

Suddenly he slammed his fist on the arm of the chair, rose, and began pacing back and forth. "Blast the woman!" he shouted as he threw his glass into the fireplace. "She must despise me. I know it! Yet still she persists in this insane alliance. Is her need for money so great that she would force my compliance and then submit herself as a wife to my authority? Or is her desire for a husband of equal if not greater importance in her scheme of things?"

He pondered on this for a moment, then gestured as if to brush it all away and began pacing again. "I've been a complete fool." He hesitated momentarily, searching for some other descriptive terms before settling on one more. "A bullheaded idiot!"

Brodhurst's final expletive was of such volume as to make Sir Edmund wince. "Calm down, m'boy. Never seen you in such a state before." He spoke quietly, attempting to soothe his friend into a more rational frame of mind. "The situation can't be hopeless. Surely there's something you can do."

"Nothing," the marquess said in a more normal voice. "God knows I've tried." He sighed in resignation and placed a hand on the mantel of the large fireplace, leaning forward to stare into the flames. "How could I have been so dim-witted as to allow this to happen? I was so certain it was a wise move. My man of business even assured me the earl's holdings were quite vast, his wealth a matter of record."

"Perhaps you have made a mistake," Edmund offered hopefully. "If your investigations have unearthed no irregularities, perhaps your assumptions are incorrect. On what grounds do you base them?"

"On what grounds?" Brodhurst nearly bellowed as he whirled to face his friend. "My eyes, that's what grounds. I caught them unawares. I saw what's behind the facade. My eyes did not lie to me!"

"Then perhaps there is a different reason for the circumstances you witnessed," the older man suggested.

"Dash it all, man, we've been over this before! If it had been only the earl, I could dismiss it as his eccentricity. But his daughter as well? No! Tell me, Edmund, do you know of any woman who would prefer wearing rags to fine gowns if she could afford them?" He watched as his friend shook his head, then continued. "There you have it. Mine is the only possible conclusion."

He leaned back and looked up to study the ceiling, massaging the back of his neck with long, slender fingers. "Damn little good my deductions will do now," he said softly, sighing again. "She has me, Edmund. I'm trapped. What a boneheaded dolt I was to sign a contract before examining the goods!" He slowly shook his head as he continued to pace.

"Won't help to keep berating yourself for a mistake of the past," Edmund consoled. "Although I myself have wondered in which direction your wits had flown when you put a pen to that paper. Could you perchance have anticipated the marriage with no little degree of pleasure?"

Brodhurst turned sharply. "You're wide of the mark there. It was all strictly business on my part."

He began pacing again as if by such actions he could demonstrate the inaccuracy of his friend's statement. Inwardly, however, he was shaken by its truth. He *had* been looking forward to the marriage. Something about the Lady Alicia had always affected him.

The girl had been such an awkward, shy young thing when he first met her, not yet pretty, but with the promise of great beauty upon maturity. He remembered her chin, a sign of inner strength, jutting out at times in rebellion against the many restrictions placed upon young, unmarried ladies in their first Season. Her eyes had always seemed to dance, revealing an intense joy of life. She had stood out in vivid relief from the insipid young ladies who made their come-out with her. He had been absolutely certain, when signing the agreement, that she would make the kind of wife for which he had been searching, with a little help and guidance from him, of course.

It's as if I were in love! he thought, amazed at his own insight. In love with an idea only, of course. Certainly not reality. At that moment his lordship was called away from his disquieting line of thought by Edmund's comforting voice. He turned gratefully to face the older gentleman.

"Didn't you hear me, Jonathan? I said you mustn't give up hope. Perhaps something will turn up later. You're not a bridegroom yet, you know."

"True," the marquess agreed, "but unless the lady changes her mind, my happy state of bachelorhood will soon disappear, and, I might add, a good deal of my money as well." Suddenly a glimmer of hope began to shine in his eyes, for an idea had come to him as he spoke. "By Jove, I've got it!" he exclaimed. "My fate lies in the hands of Lady Alicia, therefore she must be persuaded to change her mind."

"And how do you propose to accomplish such a feat?" Edmund asked, clearly interested in this new approach. "Certainly not with an appeal to her better nature, I hope."

"No, of course not. I haven't lost all sense, dear friend," he replied, a slight smile returning to his previously strained features. "But if there were a suitor more to her liking, perhaps she might release me in his favor."

"She might at that," Edmund agreed. "But I can't help thinking it's not quite the thing to foist your problems on some other poor, unsuspecting chap. Devilish bad ton, Jonathan, I must say."

"Have no fear," the marquess reassured his friend. "I have no intention of sacrificing someone else to save myself. You see, once I've obtained my own release, a new contract must needs be drawn. I have no doubt the other gentleman involved will discover the lady's true character and motive before such a contract can be signed. If not, I shall see to it that he is not entrapped. She will then need to look for someone new. When I finish spreading my tale, she will be forced to settle for some wealthy cit, if she can find one who will have her. It's not one bit more than she deserves."

Suddenly, he felt much better. He rang for the butler and asked for a full decanter of brandy. When it arrived, his lordship poured himself a drink and refilled Edmund's glass.

"A toast, my friend," he said, holding his glass high. "A toast to my freedom which I hope will be obtained soon." He emptied his glass in one swallow, then refilled it immediately, a look of satisfaction on his face.

Edmund had only sipped his brandy. Examining his glass with a slightly worried expression, he asked the question which had been bothering him for some time. "Whom did you have in mind to take your place?"

The question took his lordship aback for a moment. "Why, I hadn't quite gotten around to that point yet. It's a bit sticky, I must say." At his friend's nod, he continued, voicing his thoughts as they came to him. "He must be some young lad who will appear to be easy prey for m'lady. Of course he must needs be wealthy, or at least have great expectations."

Both men were silent for a moment, searching their minds for friends or acquaintances who might meet the requirements just mentioned. "What about that young chap who escorted Lady Alicia and her aunt yesterday on Rotten Row?" Brodhurst asked, snapping his fingers. "He seemed devoted to the lady, and is, if I'm not mistaken, quite well born."

"You mean Geoffrey Baugh, I believe," Sir Edmund replied. "Seems a good lad, though I'd not met him before, so I can't say of a certainty. But his family is good. His father is the Earl of Selcester. In fact, he'd be a perfect choice for your scheme, since I'd swear he's smitten with the lady already. Unfortunately there's no money in that direction. He's the sixth son, and will probably inherit only a pittance."

"Ah," Brodhurst interjected, "but what if the lady were unaware of his lack of fortune? To one who has nothing, any inheritance can appear enticing."

"You would lie to her, then?" Edmund asked with a look of disapproval quite apparent on his normally pleasant features.

"Of course not," the younger man replied calmly. "Lord

Granville lied to me, but I shall not return it in kind. No, the information will not come from me. I cannot even hint at such a thing. She would suspect *my* words." He pondered the problem a few moments. "You will just have to impart that information for me, my friend." He looked around expectantly.

"Oh, no." Edmund answered forcefully with a vigorous shake of his head. "You're not including me in your scheming. I refuse to become involved. Absolutely refuse!"

"But Edmund," his lordship said with a stricken look in his eyes, "you must help me. My situation is desperate. Will you condemn me to a life of wretchedness? I had no idea our friendship meant so little to you."

"You know better than that, m'boy. Our friendship is not in question at the moment, but rather my honor. I will help if I can, rest assured. But lying? No!" The older gentleman answered with such finality that Brodhurst refrained from pressing further.

"Very well. Perhaps a few rumors in the proper circles will do just as well. Indeed, it might even be a better route. To have such information come to her from a completely disinterested source would serve my purpose magnificently."

Edmund nodded in agreement, then cleared his throat in a rather nervous manner. "I have something to tell you, Brodhurst. Perhaps I should have mentioned it earlier. My apologies. Fact of the matter is I've been planning to call at Wynford House myself. Lady Matilda has most graciously invited me. I met her years ago, you know, before she married Ludlow. I confess I was surprised she remembered me."

Brodhurst's amazed expression was quickly turning to one of calculation. "Famous, dear fellow! Nothing could be better. Using the pretext of dancing attendance upon the Lady Alicia, you could keep me apprised of her actions. It's a perfect position to ascertain immediately if she displays an interest in someone else."

"I suppose I could accommodate you there. Must confess I've a decided curiosity about the lady. There seems to be an air of mystery about her. Probably due to the veil and all. Piqued my interest a bit, however."

"It's settled then," Brodhurst announced. "You satisfy your curiosity and aid a friend-in-need at the same time." He threw his arm over the older man's shoulder and walked him to the door. "The fates sent you to my side, my friend. I feel as if I've been given a reprieve. You have my eternal gratitude." He spoke softly, sincerity evident in both his voice and his eyes.

Sir Edmund appeared slightly embarrassed. "Better to wait until I've actually accomplished something," he mumbled and quickly took his leave.

The marquess, spirits flying high, was of the opinion that events were moving in a favorable direction. His earlier air of dejection vanished, and he removed to his room where, with the expert help of his valet, he prepared himself properly for a visit to White's that afternoon.

Sir Edmund, with no little amount of trepidation, set out toward Cavendish Square. After ascending the steps at Wynford House, he was ushered by the butler into the drawing room. Lady Matilda was in the best of moods, having just received, from Madame Bertine, delivery of one of the most ravishing creations that modiste had ever designed for her. She had been contemplating the event to which she would wear it to best advantage, namely Lady Hargrave's ball that very evening, when Sir Edmund was announced.

"How good of you to call on us," Matilda said, smiling warmly as he bent low over her hand. "It's always a pleasure to renew old friendships. But what a pity you've come at a time when Alicia is out."

She motioned to a comfortable chair near her. "Please join me. We shall have a comfortable coze, and perhaps she'll return shortly. Would you believe she has been behaving like a tourist, dragging her maid around the entire city? Today they are visiting the Tower. Young Baugh is escorting her, and if I'm not mistaken, he seemed just as excited as my niece. I should have thought they both were too old for such things." She pursed her lips, but the smile in her eyes belied her condemnation of the activity.

"An inquisitive mind is to be commended," Edmund replied in a quiet and pleasant tone. "And I daresay such a mind need not be found only among the extremely young." His eyebrows rose, questioningly.

"How clever you are, sir. You have found me out, and I confess ignorance as to what gave me away. But I do hold a certain amount of envy for those two, for I have never visited the sights of London myself. I collect it was due to lack of will on my part that I never set out upon such an expedition.

"Oh no, dear lady," Edmund quickly replied. "Please permit me to contradict you, for I cannot allow you to demean yourself so. I am convinced it was not a lack of will, but merely a lack of proper companionship. Pray allow *me* to escort you to any site of interest you might be inclined to visit."

Matilda looked at her charming visitor with a most engaging twinkle in her eye. "I confess, sir, to an unrequited desire to visit the botanical gardens."

A light sprang to Sir Edmund's eyes as he recognized a kindred spirit, and soon the two were deep in the discussion of plants in general, and roses in particular.

When Alicia arrived on the arm of young Mr. Baugh, she found her aunt in high spirits—a broad smile on her lips, and a light in her eyes that Alicia seldom had seen before. Sir Edmund also appeared more animated than she had first thought him. Upon meeting him in Hyde Park, she had been distinctly impressed with his cool and aloof attitude, thinking it was one of disapproval. Now the reserve was gone, and he seemed pleased to be in their presence.

She handed her pelisse to the footman and advanced into the drawing room. Lifting her veil, she allowed Sir Edmund to view her features clearly. This man was an intimate of Brodhurst, and she was convinced the marquess had slandered her scandalously. She would be interested to see Sir Edmund's reaction. But the gentleman's eyebrow lifted only slightly, and his greeting was unexceptional.

"Permit me, my lady, to say it's too bad of you to hide such charming features behind a veil."

"I hide only from the sun, sir," she replied stiffly.

"There may be those who would think otherwise," Sir Edmund said meaningfully, his eyes searching her face.

"I daresay you are correct, but I have no time to bother with individuals who jump to false conclusions before ascertaining all the facts. Such foolish actions have been known to cause great pain, a fact to which I personally can attest." Her voice was quite cool and objective in tone, but her eyes momentarily betrayed the depth of her emotions before resuming their polite but disinterested gaze.

"Getting a bit too serious, aren't you?" Geoffrey commented, looking first at Alicia and then Sir Edmund. "It's been too grand a day to spoil it now, don't you think?"

Alicia flashed a smile in his direction, grateful for the diversion, and immediately disclaimed any possibility of an argument. But Sir Edmund was not to leave off quite so easily. With a piercing look, he caught Alicia by surprise.

"Remember, my dear, such people as we have described often bring even greater suffering upon themselves. Perhaps they should be pitied rather than punished." Having delivered this comment in a soft voice, he then turned calmly to the younger gentleman and began to quiz him about their outing.

Alicia had no time to ponder Sir Edmund's last remark, disquieting though it was, for she was immediately drawn into the conversation, a description of her impressions of the Tower being requested by Lady Matilda. She owned to having experienced a certain amount of revulsion at the gruesome history of the place, but was still pleased to have visited it.

As the conversation continued, Alicia admitted to a preference for a more pleasant destination at the next outing. Sir Edmund immediately suggested a visit to Curtis's Botanical Gardens might be just the thing to restore her, and that perhaps he and Lady Matilda might join them. The idea was received most enthusiastically, and Alicia and Geoffrey immediately set about planning the excursion. Matilda joined in happily, casting a grateful glance toward Sir Edmund, who smiled broadly in return. After an animated discussion, it was decided the expedition should be accomplished seven days hence, and that a picnic be included in the day's activities.

"A most agreeable afternoon," Matilda announced after the gentlemen had taken their leave. "I do believe our visit to the gardens will be quite enjoyable."

"Why, Aunt Matilda," Alicia exclaimed. "I first thought your agreement to accompany us was merely related to your position as chaperon. But I now see you are actually anticipating the excursion with pleasure. I would not have thought it of you," she said in mock surprise, then quickly hugged her aunt happily.

"Oh, my dear, you have no idea how often in the past I have secretly desired to tour London's places of interest, just as you are doing now. But with age there comes a dampening of one's more childish wishes. I own, if Sir Edmund had not forced the issue, I would not be accompanying you this trip. So kind of him, don't you think?" She stopped for a moment, then clasped her hands enthusiastically. "Oh, but it will be such fun, don't you agree?"

Alicia, touched by her aunt's obvious pleasure, nodded in agreement, kissed her quickly on the cheek, and commented on her own anticipation of the outing. The fact that she herself would have preferred a visit to the museum was not evident, either in her voice or expression. The two ladies began to plan their attire with such enthusiasm that a stranger might have thought them both fresh out of the schoolroom.

Matilda finally reverted to her more practical nature, however, and reminded her niece of the Hargraves' ball that evening. "You should rest, dear, for I have no doubt the evening will prove to be a strain. This is your first ball since your previous Season, and I fully expect you to emerge a success. I own a rest would do me some benefit, also. I had no idea planning an excursion could be so tiring."

Alicia reluctantly agreed to rest, and the ladies ascended the stairs together, brought close in a bond of friendship as well as of blood. Before entering her room, however, she remembered her initial conversation with Sir Edmund, and expressed her opinion that he seemed to have grasped their intent in regard to the marquess.

"I collect he will immediately inform his lordship, and our little plan of revenge will be at an end."

"It doesn't signify," Matilda countered, totally unmoved by her niece's obvious concern. "If the marquess learns of his mistake and has both the manners and backbone to apologize, you can release him with the knowledge that he has both suffered and learned a great deal. Unfortunately, if I'm not mistaken, his lordship will not so easily be swayed from his original opinion, and will continue to suffer as a result. In any event, we need do nothing more. He will punish himself. We have only supplied the instrument." She smiled and patted her niece's hand comfortingly. "Don't worry, my dear. Put the marquess out of your mind. Think only of enjoying yourself this evening. You will, you know. I'm convinced of it."

Matilda happily turned to enter her own room, and Alicia closed her door slowly, wishing with all her heart that she could put Lord Brodhurst out of her thoughts completely. Unfortunately, he seemed to own a permanent space at the back of her mind and was prone to pop out on almost any occasion. She recalled how he had occupied her thoughts during her visit to the Tower, and she smiled, remembering how strong had been her sudden desire to see him imprisoned in that august edifice. Yet now, after conversing with Sir Edmund, the thought of his lordship suffering at her hands was vaguely disturbing. She shook off the strange feeling and rang for

Mary to help her disrobe, for the luxury of an afternoon nap had suddenly become quite appealing.

Only a few hours later, Matilda knocked gently and entered her niece's room in order to inspect the young lady prior to their departure for the ball. She herself was dressed most becomingly in peach sarsenet over cream satin, with the exquisite Ludlow diamonds gracing her neck and earlobes.

Alicia had chosen blue, her favorite color, to match her eyes. A gown of deep blue satin was covered by white spider gauze with tiny diamante scattered in shimmering clusters like stars. The neckline was extremely décolleté, displaying more than a hint of well-formed bosom. Tiny puffed sleeves and long gloves set off fine-boned shoulders and graceful arms. A single sapphire hung from a golden chain around her neck, with smaller sapphire drops at her ears. Her hair was braided in a crown, with blue satin ribbon wound through it.

"My dear, you are absolutely lovely," Matilda exclaimed. "There is no doubt in my mind but that you will take this town by storm." She continued to walk around her niece, nodding and smiling in approval. Only when she looked at her niece's hair did her smile fade. "I would prefer a different style," she commented almost to herself, "but no matter, this becomes you nicely."

In the meantime Alicia had been looking at her aunt in astonishment. Never had she seen Lady Matilda looking so young and glowing. She suddenly realized her aunt's sacrifice—the loss of ten years of her youth to a quiet life in the country as companion to her brother and substitute mother to his child. Alicia was filled with gratitude for all that had happened, since it had resulted in their coming to London and was thus bringing happiness to someone she loved deeply.

Upon being informed that the carriage was waiting, the ladies proceeded down the stairs, smiling and chatting easily, as if such an elegant evening was a common occurrence in their lives. Alicia was surprised that she did not tense as the carriage approached the Hargrave residence. She was excited, as was to be expected, but kept a feeling of assurance and competency to withstand the scrutiny of every important personage who might be present. Perhaps it was the gown, her aunt's presence, or her increased age, but whatever the cause, she knew she would never again suffer in awkward shyness as she had done nearly three years ago.

The affair was quickly becoming a sad crush, and Alicia had to admit to some degree of discomfort and nervousness as they slowly ascended the curved stairway to greet their hostess and enter the ballroom. Her mouth was unaccustomedly dry and her heartbeat markedly increased. Perhaps her eyes betrayed some slight amount of anxiety, for at that moment Matilda touched her hand in a reassuring manner. Alicia could not help but smile and hold her head high in response to her aunt's encouragement.

Such a proud bearing and pleasant smile must have greatly impressed Lady Hargrave, for she nodded and smiled her approval after scrutinizing the young lady carefully. Her greeting was most cordial, even though she gently admonished both ladies for absenting themselves from London's social scene for far too long.

Matilda was most gratified. It seemed all her hopes for Alicia were to be fulfilled. She was fortunate enough to overhear Lady Hargrave whispering to her closest confidant that Mrs. Montrose would find her daughter, Susan, whom all expected to be the rage, was soon to be outshone by the lovely Lady Alicia Granville.

As they stepped into the ballroom, the lady in question felt momentary panic. The light of hundreds of candles reflected and refracted by the myriad facets of the cut crystal chandeliers was dazzling. The room was crowded with exquisitely coifed and bejeweled ladies in lovely gowns, and gentlemen of all ages, impressively dressed in evening attire, some even appearing to outshine the ladies they escorted.

Alicia felt a familiar feeling of being unable to compete

with all the lovely ladies well up within her. She had experienced it all before, and had deemed herself a failure. Her momentary lapse of self-confidence was just that, however—only momentary. For Geoffrey Baugh, who had stationed himself near the door with the express purpose, it seemed, of being the first to greet Alicia, stepped forward immediately and made his presence known.

Even though he had prevailed upon her to promise him a dance that very afternoon while they perused the Royal Armory of Henry VIII, anyone of even moderate acumen could foresee that the young lady would be the center of a large circle of attentive young men at the ball, and therefore likely to forget such a minor commitment. Prudence would dictate that any gentleman wishing to escort the lady onto the dance floor be among the first to request that honor before her card was filled. Mr. Baugh was definitely no slowtop.

Alicia was visibly pleased to see him, and quickly agreed to accompany the young gentleman in the country dance which was just beginning. Geoffrey held himself proudly erect as he led her onto the dance floor, as if he were aware of all the pairs of eyes watching their progress with extreme interest and even envy.

Alicia was definitely a shining star of the evening. Her dress was not only becoming but also striking in both cut and color, definitely a step above the usual gowns worn the the *jeunes filles* making their come-out that Season. Yet her innocence and freshness was quite apparent and set her apart from the more mature ladies who were considered well entrenched in the ton.

Lady Matilda watched the young couple for a moment, smiling in approval of her protégée. Then she turned and slowly made her way to an area where most dowagers could be found. A deep, pleasant voice arrested her forward motion, and caused her to look up into the smiling eyes of Sir Edmund.

"Pray, my lady, do not tell me that you plan to hide such charm for the entire evening seated among the chaperons, finding excitement only in hearing the latest *on-dits*." He smiled and bowed, kissing her hand in a magnificent fashion.

"Why, Sir Edmund, certainly you must be aware that I'm of an age where that is the most appropriate place for me. I've enjoyed my Season, let the young enjoy theirs." She spoke gaily, turning to watch the dancers, her eyes alight with pleasure. "Doesn't Alicia look lovely?" she asked proudly. "I own watching her makes me feel young again."

"Then certainly one with youth reborn should not waste it among the dowagers," he said in mock formality, a small smile playing at the corner of his mouth. Then, in all seriousness, he offered his arm. "Shall we join the dancers?"

Matilda hesitated only a moment, then smiled sweetly and, with a twinkle in her eye, accepted his offer. She laughed gaily as Sir Edmund commented she could not have regained her youth that evening, for it was his decided opinion she had never lost it.

On the dance floor, he continued his gallantry, remarking on her grace, and disbelieving her protestations that she had not danced for years. As she recalled the hours spent practicing in her room, she colored charmingly, bringing a responsive gleam of appreciation, if not indeed a certain fondness, to Sir Edmund's eyes.

Alicia watched as Sir Edmund led her aunt onto the floor. Although involved in a dance herself, she was given ample opportunity to survey her surroundings, for Mr. Baugh had once again lapsed into a daze much like the condition he had demonstrated upon first meeting her. His relapse took her quite unawares. Their outings together had led Alicia to believe that they had developed a comfortable friendship, and she had been more than happy to give him the first dance. But as she took his arm, he mumbled something about normal conversation seeming near to sacrilege when in the presence of a goddess. After that, he accomplished the intricate steps of the dance quite competently, but all the time doing so in silence, his mouth slightly open and a look of pure adoration in his eyes.

Alicia had begun to feel distinctly uncomfortable, and looked to the other dancers to provide her with some diversion. The sight of her aunt laughing gaily as she danced was a pleasant surprise, but it also gave rise to a certain feeling of unease as she became aware that her aunt might be developing a *tendre* for Sir Edmund. She decided she must become better acquainted with the gentleman, so that she could protect her aunt from any unnecessary pain if he proved unworthy of Lady Matilda's sweet nature.

To this end, at the conclusion of the dance, she hurriedly led Mr. Baugh across the room to station herself by Matilda's side. Geoffrey found his voice upon seeing Sir Edmund, and became quite talkative in the midst of the small but congenial group. Unfortunately, he had developed a distressing habit of trailing off in midsentence whenever his glance included the fair Alicia. In exasperation, she sent him on an errand to procure her a glass of lemonade. As he left, she turned back to her aunt in relief.

"I'm sure I don't know what has gotten into him," she commented, her displeasure evident in the tiny furrow visible in her brow.

"You mustn't think too harshly of the poor boy, dear," Matilda said, amused. "You should be greatly flattered by his silence. He does seem to be quite smitten by you."

"Well, I must say I would prefer a lively conversation to his silent display of appreciation. Talking with oneself can become boring, I assure you. I own his silence quite spoiled our dance." Her sidelong glance at Sir Edmund prompted the gentleman to remedy the situation.

"My dear young lady, won't you allow me to partner you in this next dance?" He offered his arm, his face composed and serious, but his eyes alight in amusement. "I promise to do my best to enliven our steps with appropriate dialogue."

Alicia, pleased to have an opportunity to examine the

gentleman more closely, smiled graciously and accepted. As they joined the other couples, he spoke quietly but most sincerely. "My lady, I must admit to being in complete agreement with Mr. Baugh. You certainly are looking most charming this evening, you know."

Alicia glanced up at him quickly, but caught no hint of mockery. She thanked him prettily, but added she considered herself to be no better than average, and in truth felt somewhat subdued in the presence of so many lovely ladies. "I own, they cast one quite into the shade," she said softly.

Edmund scrutinized her carefully, as if trying to determine if her modesty were genuine. Her guileless eyes stared up at him, and he could not resist smiling in return. "Have no fear, young lady, you are definitely above average in this company or any other." He looked around at the guests crowded into the ballroom as he spoke. "If my eyes don't deceive me, a great many acquaintances of mine are watching us at this very moment, and I daresay at the end of the dance, I shall be inundated with requests for an introduction."

"To me?" Alicia asked, astonished.

"Why, of course," he replied, bemused by her reaction. "Certainly you've experienced such a situation before? You did have your first Season some time ago, I believe."

"Yes, of course I did," she replied, perplexed. "But there certainly was no rush to obtain introductions. In fact, there was one instance of a certain gentleman who allowed my acquaintance to slip completely from his mind." She spoke lightly, unwilling to admit to the pain which that particular memory still evoked within her.

"Oh?" he remarked. "I would rather have thought you to be the one to forget an introduction." He gazed at her searchingly.

She blushed, remembering how she had pretended just such a thing in defense against Lord Brodhurst's faulty memory. "I confess to pretending forgetfulness on one occasion, but only to protect myself—" She stopped suddenly, realizing she was about to open her past to the scrutiny of a near-stranger. She had intended to extract information from Sir Edmund, but found the reverse actually happening. Undoubtedly, he was there merely to spy for his friend, the marquess. She shook herself inwardly and smiled up at her partner. "It doesn't signify. That happened almost three years ago, and I admit to having changed somewhat since then."

Sir Edmund lifted an eyebrow and grinned. "That is an understatement, my dear. Definitely an understatement."

The dance ended, and Alicia returned to find her aunt deep in conversation with an elegantly gowned lady of increased years. The stranger looked up as Matilda performed the introductions.

"Lady Castlereagh, may I present my niece, Alicia."

The two exchanged polite greetings, and this was followed by close scrutiny from the older lady, who then smiled, nodding approval as she turned to Lady Matilda. "You're correct about the hairstyle, my dear. I'll send my dresser to you, and she will see to it the girl's hair is perfection. Otherwise your niece is a gem, a diamond of the first water. I don't believe I've ever seen such fine skin, such a clear and delicate complexion. I'm simply too envious for words."

Alicia, realizing she was in the presence of one of the patronesses of Almack's and a powerful member of the ton, had stood quietly during the examination and was pleased yet slightly embarrassed by the compliments. She thanked the lady pleasantly, and joined in a discussion of the joys of country living as compared to the pleasures afforded the London dweller.

Lady Castlereagh soon took her leave, promising to send vouchers to them the following day, and proclaiming that Alicia would soon be the rage of all London.

Matilda was pleased at the results of the meeting, confident that barring unforeseen incidents, her niece's success in the ton was assured. She was soon renewing old friendships and found herself partnered on the dance floor more than a little. That is, when she wasn't occupied performing introductions to the lovely young lady in her charge.

Alicia found Sir Edmund's words to be quite prophetic. He approached her often during the evening, with eager young—and sometimes not so young—gentlemen at his side, anxious to make her acquaintance. Mr. Baugh also was constantly hovering near. His ability to converse had apparently returned, and his stature was much increased as he found himself envied for having been honored by the first dance with the enchanting Lady Alicia.

Matilda had just finished an enjoyable but rather stately country dance with an old friend of her late husband's when she became aware of Lady Sanderson's shrill tones.

"My dear Matilda, I'm sure I'm most fortunate to have an opportunity to greet you, for I've been awaiting a time when you were not surrounded by so many old friends and well-wishers, and I had despaired of ever having a word with you, for it seemed that you would never be allowed a free moment, yet here you are, alone at last, just when I had given up all hope." The older lady stopped her speech only long enough for Matilda to give her a pleasant greeting, and then continued in her irritating tones.

"I must say that I'm most pleased to see my godchild enjoying herself so much this evening, for I own I would never have thought that our little Alicia would develop into such a charming young lady and take so well, as she most certainly has this evening, especially since she experienced such a disastrous first Season. But of course, that was quite some time ago, and she has matured a great deal, but . . ." Her voice trailed off as she stared at the couples whirling past them, her expression one of shock and disapproval.

"Oh my, is that Alicia dancing with Viscount Belham?" Lady Sanderson asked. Without waiting for confirmation, she continued quickly, "But, of course that is she, but really, my dear Matilda, it simply mustn't be!" Her voice became louder and more strident as her agitation increased. "Alicia should not be waltzing. She has never been granted approval!"

With those fateful words, all conversation around them ceased, and eyes turned to watch the young lady twirl by, happily oblivious to the intense scrutiny she was receiving.

# = 6 =

LADY MATILDA, SHOCKED AS much by Lady Sanderson's indiscretion in loudly proclaiming Alicia's social blunder as by the information itself, moved quickly to silence her companion. "Oh, I'm quite certain you must be mistaken," she said, loudly enough to be heard by those who were straining their ears to gather more information about this new and seemingly delicious bit of gossip. "You must have forgotten, my dear. After all, almost three years have passed since her last Season, so great has been her partiality for life in the country." Her expression was so severe that Lady Sanderson came to realize the damage she had wrought and began to stammer, her voice trailing off as she glanced about. With an ashen face and gushing her apologies, she quickly left Matilda's side, allowing the widow to set her mind to contemplating a way out of the unfortunate muddle.

Alicia continued to enjoy the dance. Her partner, although not exceptional, was quite adequate, and of course the waltz was her favorite. She was smiling and chatting gaily as they turned around the room. Suddenly her heart sank, and she stifled a tiny gasp after spying a latecomer strolling through the door.

Viscount Belham, aware that his partner's interest had wandered, looked over to discover the reason. "Oh, it's Brodhurst," he declared flatly, a look of resignation on his face. "Most fortunate I had this dance before he arrived. I collect you would like to meet him."

"No, thank you," she replied coldly, turning her face from the door. 'I've already had that dubious pleasure." The set of her mouth was enough to convince anyone of her sincerity, and she was completely unaware of the surprised but pleased expression which appeared on her partner's face as she spoke those words.

The strains of the waltz died away. Alicia politely thanked the viscount and excused herself, heading toward her aunt. It was time for an early departure from the affair, for she did not relish meeting Lord Brodhurst again. Oh! It was so typical of the man to have appeared and spoil an otherwise perfect evening for her, not to mention bringing her little revenge plot to a premature conclusion.

She fanned herself busily to give credence to her headlong rush toward the ladies clustered at the side of the room. Most would surmise she was merely overheated, not fleeing from one of the most eligible bachelors of the ton. And yet she felt a sudden spark of desire to have the marquess see her as the other gentlemen had, a lovely and entrancing young lady. She extinguished the spark with the thought that once having viewed her without a veil, he would still consider her beneath his notice. She tapped her fan in vexation at her own foolishness. Why should she care a twig what that particular gentleman thought of her now?

She put aside such disquieting thoughts as she discovered her aunt already making preparations to leave the ball. The widow appeared quite calm, but Alicia could detect a hint of anxiety in her eyes. Perhaps she had also seen the marquess enter.

"Oh, there you are, my dear. I was just to the point of sending for you. Our carriage has been ordered, and we must take our leave of Lady Hargrave."

Lady Matilda looked decidedly pale. Her fingers trembled as she caught Alicia's hand in both of hers. Surely the presence of the marquess could not have caused such distress. She touched her aunt's arm gently, her eyes full of worry.

"What has happened? Are you ill?"

"Why yes, you might say that," Matilda replied enigmatically. "I have decided to suffer a severe headache, and it will grow to such proportions that I simply cannot stay longer. Allow me to take your arm, my dear, for I am prepared to grow weaker by the moment."

Alicia did as she was told, thoroughly bemused by the entire situation. She had never before seen her aunt act so strangely, but her air of enforced calm led the younger lady to believe it imperative that she say nothing and follow along, no matter what her aunt might say or do.

As they approached their hostess, Lady Hargrave noticed that something was amiss and was most solicitous when told of Lady Matilda's unfortunate megrim. The two ladies said their goodbyes, then quietly slipped out the door and down the stairs, relieved to see their carriage had already been brought round.

Matilda broke the silence immediately upon seating herself in the Brougham. "I'm sure I don't know what possessed that woman!" she snapped in exasperation. "Why, she practically shouted it to the entire room. If it had been her express purpose to cause mischief, she could not have succeeded better!"

"What woman?" Alicia asked, attempting to discover the cause of her aunt's extreme agitation. "What has happened?" Her questions finally penetrated Matilda's distraction, and she explained the problem, chiding herself as well as her niece for having neglected such an important point as obtaining approval before waltzing in public.

"Oh, Aunt Matilda, I'm so very sorry. I had quite forgotten," Alicia said softly.

Matilda patted her niece's hand and smiled reassuringly. "Don't apologize to me, dear, for I fear it is you who will suffer as a result." She paused for a moment, her expression unreadable in the darkness. Then she continued, her voice full of determination. "We simply must find a way around this muddle. It's so distressing. And to have it happen at your first ball of this Season is simply inexcusable. Oh, I do so wish your godmother would learn to curb her tongue!"

"Yes," Alicia agreed. "She has always been one to prattle on, with little thought of the effect her words might have. But I cannot bring myself to consider the situation as being so very serious. Certainly I am no young miss fresh out of the schoolroom. And—" she added emphatically, "this is not my first Season."

"But it might as well be," Matilda countered. "Your first visit to London was extremely short and over two years ago as well. Many are regarding this Season as the continuation of your come-out. To fly in the face of tradition by waltzing without approval may result in your being denied vouchers to Almack's!"

Alicia grew silent as she realized the full import of those words. To have the doors of Almack's closed to her could also mean that she might be denied access to the highest circles of the ton.

The two ladies completed the ride to Cavendish Square in silence, each contemplating a possible solution to the problem. Upon arriving at Wynford House, they refused a light supper and repaired to their respective bedrooms, hoping that the morning might bring them insight and inspiration.

Alicia lay in her bed unable to sleep. She was deeply worried about her immediate problem of the unauthorized waltz, but she also found herself once again considering the odious marquess who, all too often of late, had risen unbidden to her thoughts. In the privacy of her bedroom, she had to admit that her glimpse of him earlier that evening had caused her pulse to quicken in a rather pleasant fashion, a fact which she could only deplore. She reminded herself that she despised the gentleman and that she found him quite conceited, selfish, and spoiled.

She also wondered at her reaction to Sir Edmund. Realizing she had been all too ready to discuss some of her most intimate problems with him, Alicia pondered why he should so evoke her trust and confidence. It was almost as if she thought of him as an uncle. Most definitely he should be considered dangerously charming, she concluded, and mentally promised herself to warn Matilda of her suspicions immediately upon arising. When sleep did come, it was less than peaceful. Even in her dreams she could not escape the exasperating Marquess of Brodhurst and the strange emotions he elicited within her.

Upon awakening early the next morning, her problem of the night before still unsolved, Alicia decided upon a ride in the park. She hoped the exercise would help to clear her mind and thus aid her in finding a solution to her difficulties.

A short time later she was attired jauntily in her blue velvet riding habit and astride Starfire, riding down the row at a gentle walk, her groom dutifully in attendance. This morning she did not chafe at the slow pace, for her mind was occupied with two problems: the predicament in which she found herself as a result of her unsanctioned waltz the night before and the peculiar flutter within her bosom whenever she thought of Lord Brodhurst.

She loosened her veil, lifting it from her face and tucking it back over the brim of her hat, for that way she felt less confined and was able to enjoy the cool, fresh air more fully. She knew that her skin was still delicate, easily damaged by the sun even on a cloudy morning, but it was very early and she promised herself only a few minutes of freedom before returning the veil to its proper position.

In good time, just as she had hoped, the morning airing astride her beloved roan worked to restore her good spirits, and she started to urge Starfire to a faster gait. This was not accomplished, however, for at that moment she was greeted by another rider on the row, Viscount Belham.

"Good morning, Lady Alicia. I had no idea you enjoyed such an early ride. Most fortunate for me, I must say." He had approached her at a brisk trot and adeptly turned his mount, slowing it to match her pace.

Alicia smiled and greeted him, no longer feeling the need to be alone. "As it happens, Lord Belham, it was my practice to rise early at Wynford Manor and ride almost every morning. Unfortunately this is only my second opportunity to exercise my mare since arriving in London, and the very first opportunity to do so at an early hour. I see, however, that few others share our interest in such activity. The row is positively deserted."

Lord Belham smiled. "Few feel the urge for exercise after a late night of entertainment," he remarked, then glanced up at the sound of another rider approaching. "Ah, here comes Brodhurst. He is one of the hardy souls."

Alicia, somewhat alarmed at the approach of the odious marquess, prudently lowered her veil. She fervently wished for some pretext upon which to excuse herself before the rider joined them, but could think of nothing in time.

Lord Brodhurst pulled in his mount at the viscount's greeting. "Good morning, Belham. Surprised to find you up at this hour. Thought you had planned a late night at the club."

The younger man grinned sheepishly. "Plans often change. Sadly enough, it was apparent from the first that fortune chose to smile on someone else last evening. I quit the game early."

Brodhurst nodded. "A wise decision. I've done the same several times."

"I believe you are acquainted with Lady Alicia Granville," the viscount said, gesturing toward his veiled companion.

Brodhurst's greeting was quite civil. That he should seem so unperturbed at this chance meeting was more than a little vexing to Alicia. She had expected, and was prepared to defend herself against, one of his verbal barbs. That he should instead smile at her in such a charming manner was positively exasperating. In retaliation she only nodded and returned her attention to the viscount.

"Our chat last evening was most enjoyable," she commented.

Unused, as he was, to such attention, especially when he found himself in the company of Lord Brodhurst, young Belham beamed his appreciation and straightened himself in the saddle. " 'Twas my pleasure, dear lady."

"Ah, so you were in attendance at the Hargraves' ball," Brodhurst interjected. "I was informed that you were present, but unfortunately our paths did not cross."

Alicia swallowed quickly, her heart skipping a beat. Such a statement revealed he had been looking for her, to what purpose she could not fathom. If he had found her, however, the result would have been an immediate and decided end to her little masquerade. That it could end shortly merely as a result of Sir Edmund's report to the marquess did not signify. She must needs deal with the immediate problem, not worry about future difficulties. Those she would handle at a later time.

"I left early, my lord," she responded. "Unfortunately my aunt, with whom I attended the affair, became unexpectedly ill."

Both gentlemen expressed polite concern, forcing her to explain further. "Thankfully, she merely suffered a megrim. The attack was severe, but short-lived. By the time we arrived home she was feeling much better, I assure you."

Alicia did not mention the cause of her aunt's sudden attack. Perhaps Brodhurst had not yet been made aware of her social solecism. Since Viscount Belham had been the partner with whom she had committed her inadvertent breach of etiquette, she deeply regretted having brought up the subject in the first place, for she feared that if the marquess had heard, he might be cruel enough to mention her embarrassment. She was deeply thankful when he did not pursue the subject, but rather took his leave politely and cantered away, leaving behind him a young lady even more annoyed for having misjudged him.

Upon returning to her house and removing her habit, with Mary's help, Alicia donned a yellow morning dress and went in search of her aunt. She found Matilda calmly sipping coffee in the breakfast room while sorting through a stack of invitations, placing those she wished to accept on a small silver tray. No sign of worry was noticeable in her serene expression which quickly changed to one of warm welcome as she spied her niece.

Alicia, normally ravenous after a morning ride, was still somewhat upset by her brief encounter with Lord Brodhurst and had no appetite. She poured herself a cup of coffee and selected a muffin from the sideboard before seating herself opposite her companion. She quietly watched her aunt examine the cards and invitations until her curiosity would allow no further delay. She asked, in a hopeful tone of voice, if Matilda had perchance come upon a satisfactory plan of action which might neutralize the damage wrought to her reputation the previous evening, explaining she had spent a less than restful night trying unsuccessfully to come upon a plan of her own.

Matilda set her lips in a firm line and announced she deemed it best that they should do nothing. "We must go on as if Lady Sanderson had not uttered a word," she said simply.

"But everyone heard her," Alicia countered in exasperation. "You yourself said she practically shouted it to the entire room."

"Quite so," Matilda agreed, "but everyone makes mistakes, you know, and Lady Sanderson's tongue has been known to run away with her before. If we behave as if nothing untoward has happened, it is my belief that everyone will accept the affair as merely due to faulty memory on your godmother's part." She smiled calmly at Alicia's amazed expression and continued. "We simply must brazen it out, my dear, for any other course would brand you guilty. After all, I'm sure you would have received permission your first Season, if you had not departed so precipitously. Our only problem is to convince Lady Sanderson that she actually *did* forget you had received that permission, for she has not the ability to dissemble in the face of the ton."

"But now that my godmother has brought me to the

attention of the patronesses, won't they realize I was never given approval?" Alicia asked quickly, her mind searching out any possible weaknesses in the plan.

"Yes, that is a distinct possibility," Matilda acknowledged, "but I am hoping that each will believe that another gave permission." Alicia felt somewhat relieved, but still had certain misgivings about being able to convince her godmother that she actually had been in error when she announced Alicia was waltzing without approval.

"I collect it would be best to call upon her as soon as possible," Alicia added, "before she complicates matters further by discussing it with others."

"I doubt we shall find it necessary to leave the house, for it's guineas to gooseberries she will pay us a morning call. Her curiosity will not allow her to waste a moment getting here."

"Oh, I pray you may be correct, for the sooner this problem is resolved, the better," Alicia said. "Perhaps then I may rest, for last night's worry left me less than refreshed this morning. I own I was of half a mind to cry off attending the costume ball tonight. It should be such fun, however, that nothing can keep me away."

Matilda looked up at the mention of the ball, a slight frown appearing on her brow. "Perhaps your first inclination was correct, dear," she spoke thoughtfully. "Such affairs can become rather risqué, and your reputation at the moment may not be strong enough to withstand another assault." She paused, noticing Alicia's surprised and disappointed reaction to her words, and continued, softening her stand somewhat. "Of course, the Bassits' annual affair has always been held in the best of taste, or so I have heard. They do not allow riffraff, as is the case at other masquerades. Otherwise I would never have considered attending in the first place."

Alicia brightened visibly. "Oh, Aunt Matilda, I do wish you will agree. Masks will be covering our faces, you know, so that we will not be recognized, and we can leave at any time you deem it improper to stay longer. Certainly we could leave before the unmasking, then no one would have the slightest inkling that we had ever attended in the first place." She watched her aunt intently as she spoke and was relieved to see the lady finally nod in agreement.

"You have a point, my dear. Perhaps I am being a trifle overcautious. I do so enjoy a masquerade. It is merely that at times it seems a mask and costume can change a person's conduct. The worst side of one's nature often appears when one feels recognition is impossible. So you must remember to be very careful and watch your actions closely."

"Oh, yes," Alicia promised quickly. "I will be most careful."

That afternoon, following the midday meal, the two ladies dawdled at the table and planned the costumes they would wear that evening. So deeply involved were they in the world of fashion that the entrance of Babcock to inform them that Lady Sanderson and Mr. Baugh were waiting in the drawing room took them completley by surprise.

Matilda rose quickly, straightening her gown and tucking an unruly tendril of hair back under her lace cap. "Well, my dear, the time has come. Remember, we must convince your godmother that approval was given during your first Season. Otherwise she will unwittingly betray us, of that I am certain." On this note of caution, she led the way down the corridor into the drawing room.

"Oh, my dears, how very good of you to see me after my abysmal actions last evening," Lady Sanderson gushed as they entered the room. "I'm sure I can't imagine what possessed me to speak as I did in the presence of the entire ton, and I simply had to come and ask your forgiveness, for you know how very attached I am to Alicia and would do nothing to harm her chances of a successful Season as this one promises to be." She breathed deeply after her lengthy pronouncement, and Matilda took advantage of the respite to calm the distraught visitor.

"There is nothing to forgive," Matilda said calmly, her statement bringing a puzzled expression to the older lady's features. "And most assuredly you have done Alicia no harm. I can't imagine how you could have thought such a thing."

Lady Sanderson looked as if she would argue the point, but Matilda turned calmly away, greeting Mr. Baugh and seeing to it that both her guests were seated comfortably. She preferred to attack the problem after Lady Sanderson had calmed herself suitably and was more amenable to the suggestion which Matilda planned to offer of her goddaughter's complete innocence.

Alicia, relieved to note that Geoffrey had reverted to his previous attitude of relaxed friendship, made a point of smiling warmly in welcome and thanking him for his support at her first ball of the Season. "I confess to having been quite relieved to see a familiar face the moment I entered the ballroom."

Obviously pleased that the charming lady appreciated his efforts even though they were prompted mainly by selfish motives, a fact he admitted only to himself, Mr. Baugh proceeded to describe the remainder of the evening's activities which Alicia had missed, including a description of the supper which had been served.

Lady Sanderson, nodding in agreement to many of young Geoffrey's observations, was unable to contain herself any longer and interrupted the young man once the supper was mentioned. "Oh, my dear, it was a lavish spread, but the ices were magnificent. Lady Hargrave is to be commended for her choice of chef, for he's French, you know, a fact which anyone who has tasted his creams cannot deny."

"I preferred the lobster patties," Geoffrey announced, reclaiming his place in the conversation. He then proceeded to express his disappointment that Alicia had left early, hoping that she had not been forced into such actions by illness.

"Oh, no," Alicia replied, smiling her appreciation of his concern. "Aunt Matilda, however, suffered an indisposition which required our leaving early. Fortunately she is much recovered this morning."

The visitors immediately focused their attention on Lady Matilda, expressing sympathy and sincere concern.

"It was nothing, really," that lady protested with a smile. "Merely a megrim which was banished easily by a proper night's rest."

"Oh, you poor dear," Lady Sanderson said in her most solicitous tone. "It's no wonder you suffered a headache after the distressing events of the evening—Alicia's glaring *faux pas* and my ungovernable tongue. . . ." The usually verbose lady trailed off in confusion as she became aware of the seemingly uncomprehending expressions of Matilda and her niece.

"But, my dear," Matilda countered gently, "a small mistake in memory on your part could not possibly have been the basis for my megrim. I'm persuaded it was the heat, unused as I am to the stuffiness of London parties."

It was Lady Sanderson's turn to display a lack of comprehension. "A mistake in memory?" she asked, astounded. "My memory? Impossible! Oh, I own you mentioned something of the like last evening, but I supposed it to be merely a covering for the careless way in which I blurted out about Alicia . . . and a most commendable effort on your part, I might add. But if you mean to stand by that premise and weather the storm, it just won't do, for everyone knows I have a most prodigious memory and could never make such a mistake." She paused, thinking over her words before amending her statement somewhat. "Of course my memory is not absolutely perfect, but it is judged extremely good by my acquaintances."

She then turned to her godchild and continued in a most sympathetic tone. "It grieves me to say this, but your only recourse is to apply to one of the hostesses, explain the entire situation in a most repentant manner, and express your regrets. Then, perhaps, you will not be barred from Almack's."

Alicia, hearing the resolve in her godmother's voice,

listened with a sinking heart. She had been aware how difficult it would be to convince the woman her memory was at fault but still had clung to a modicum of hope, knowing her aunt to be a most persuasive lady. Now it appeared all hope was lost.

Matilda, unwilling as yet to concede defeat was preparing to disagree with her guest when Babcock entered to hand her an envelope and announce that a person—he uttered the word with eyebrow raised in a most expressive manner—was demanding to see her.

Matilda quickly opened the envelope and discovered vouchers to Almack's accompanied by a note from Lady Castlereagh, which she quickly read and reread before looking up and smiling broadly. "Escort the, ah, person to my room, Babcock, and send her refreshments. I will be up shortly."

As the butler left, Matilda turned to her niece, a look of triumph spreading across her features. "Lady Castlereagh sent her dresser to style your hair, dear. She also sent vouchers and a most interesting note. It seems there was a rumor circulating last evening that you had waltzed without proper approval. She informs me that she immediately pronounced this as totally preposterous, as she herself gave such approval during your first Season, thus squelching any further discussion on the matter. Wasn't that thoughtful of Amelia?"

Matilda allowed the surprising news to be fully understood before continuing. Then, turning to Lady Sanderson, she spoke calmly. "So it appears that your prodigious memory is not perfect, my dear, as you yourself were wise to point out, and which of course is no condemnation of you, for we all make mistakes at one time or another."

Alicia, stunned at such surprising information, searched her own memory thoroughly, but without success, to pinpoint exactly when the famous hostess had sanctioned such activity on her part.

Lady Sanderson, also shocked at the contents of the note, sputtered a moment and then surrendered graciously. "Well, I must say this has certainly been a most enlightening morning. It appears I was mistaken about the waltz after all, which is no small thing I assure you, for in all the years of my adult life, this is the first time I have known my memory to fail me, at least on so important a matter. But of course it is quite wonderful for you, child," she observed with a tone of genuine pleasure. In deep self-reproach she continued, "I simply must learn to curb my tongue, mustn't I, since it nearly caused you a great deal of mischief, which you must believe I wouldn't have happen for the world, for I've always wanted only your happiness."

Alicia soothed her godmother by replying that she had always appreciated Lady Sanderson's efforts on her behalf and held her in the fondest regard. Since no harm had been done, she suggested the entire incident be forgotten, and Matilda agreed readily.

Geoffrey was probably the most relieved to see that particular topic dropped, never having fully understood why Alicia's waltzing should have prompted such a furor in the first place. Now he could converse freely with her and enjoy the time left of their morning visit. Unfortunately he was not to be treated to even a small tête-à-tête, for Lady Sanderson began speaking of a matter which affected him directly.

"Oh, I must pass on the strangest bit of tittle-tattle which was being circulated at the Hargraves' ball. This concerns you, Geoffrey, and I admit to being somewhat remiss in not mentioning it sooner, but naturally I was worried about the much more important matter involving dear Alicia, which I'm certain you'll understand. But to return to the *on-dit* I heard, it is being said that you, Geoffrey, inherited quite an easy competence, which of course I naturally denied, knowing you to be the youngest son and also that your father was not yet in that lamentable state as to be referred to as the *late* Earl of Selcester, but my objection was immediately countered with the information that you inherited from your grandmother, which of course I dismissed totally as being a Banbury tale."

She finished her lengthy discourse with an expectant glance toward Geoffrey.

"How the deuce anyone found out is beyond me," he said, looking nonplussed and a trifle embarrassed. "Owe you an apology, Lady Sanderson. Should have spoken of this sooner, but never gave it much thought."

"Are you saying that you have inherited some money?" Alicia asked, intrigued.

"Actually, the rumor was mistaken on most counts. Inherited from my great aunt, you know. Seems I was her favorite, the babe of the family and all that." He colored slightly at this revelation. "Also, I'd hardly call it an easy competence, just adequate, though of course a great deal more than I'd expect to receive from my father."

"How fortunate for you," Alicia said brightly, smiling at his apparent discomfort. "But why should you keep it a secret?"

"Oh, I had no such intention," he countered. "But the inheritance was only settled on me recently, and I hesitated to mention it lest many consider me a braggart, especially since the amount was no great fortune."

"Most proper of you," Lady Sanderson adjudged with a nod of her head.

"Yes," Matilda agreed, "but if you told no one, how did the rumor start?" Her question resulted in a sprightly discussion about the origin of rumors and their ability to travel swiftly, often arriving at a destination before the individual concerned.

"This is all very interesting, of course," Matilda concluded in a more practical tone of voice. "But now, since your inheritance is no longer a secret, your reticence in speaking of it may cause you to be judged more wealthy than you are—and therefore a most eligible prospect—by ambitious mamas. I have no doubt a great many lures will be cast out in your direction, my boy. Take care and tread warily, or you will soon find yourself dancing attendance on some young miss fresh out of the schoolroom."

"Have no fear in that regard," he assured everyone, his gaze directed steadfastly toward Alicia.

She blushed becomingly, partly from pleasure at being the focus of his attention, but also from embarrassment, since she preferred to think of him merely as a friend. In fact, she was determined to dissuade the gentleman from pursuing this line of thinking as soon as possible. Most certainly she did not want to lead him to the point of offering for her, only to dash his hopes with a refusal. For refuse she would if such a proposal were made. Her future husband must definitely be more mature. With that thought, the picture of a tall, handsome marquess flashed to her mind only to be banished immediately with the promise of a severe mental scolding as soon as she found herself alone once again.

Lady Sanderson rose, signaling an end to any further discussion within the group. The morning call was over. Leave-taking was short, and as soon as the two ladies were alone, Alicia turned to her aunt in perplexity.

"I own to having no memory of Lady Castlereagh granting approval for me to waltz."

"I have no doubt in that regard," Matilda replied with a wink and a grin, "for it is quite apparent to me that she did no such thing. She mentioned to me, however, her distinct pleasure in the transformation which has taken place since your first Season, and obviously has come to your aid without being asked, an act for which we owe her a great debt of gratitude. By acting promptly, she not only sanctioned any further waltzing on your part, but also removed any possibility of scandal from your appearance last night. I own there may be some who will guess the truth, but no one will question the word of Lady Castlereagh. In Amelia you have a most powerful friend, my dear."

Alicia, openly surprised that the lady would champion her, continued to question her aunt, knowing that seldom did such an important hostess involve herself so deeply in the lives of young newcomers to the ton.

Matilda thus was persuaded to relate her conversation

with Lady Castlereagh the previous evening, explaining that the hostess had taken a special interest in Alicia due to a friendship of many years between herself and Matilda. She had remembered Alicia's come-out, her awkward shyness, and undeveloped form.

"She even mentioned seeing Lord Brodhurst being introduced to you more than once," Matilda added.

"Oh!" Alicia gasped, coloring deeply. "I had no idea anyone else was aware of my humiliation."

"But, my dear, according to Amelia, it was not your humiliation, but rather his. She had the distinct impression that you cut him, and believes he was of the same opinion. In fact, I collect it was the one action on your part which won her to your side. She had seen so many young misses wilting in adoration merely at his glance, you see, that she was most impressed to find a young lady who practically ignored him, even to the point of forgetting a previous introduction."

Again, all that Alicia could utter was "Oh!" Her thoughts were confused, her emotions mixed. It had never occurred to her that in protecting herself from emotional pain by pretending to have no interest, she had, in fact, cut Lord Brodhurst. That she had given a set-down to the magnificent marquess without having spoken more than a few words was a new concept which she must needs ponder at greater length.

"Well, whatever the reason, I am grateful for her aid, and shall tell her so," Alicia announced in an effort to bring the conversation to an end. She then started for the stairs, planning to retire to the privacy of her room to consider all the implications of this new development. "Perhaps I should write her a short note immediately," she muttered absently.

"A note would be most acceptable, my dear," Matilda observed approvingly, "but not at this moment. Have you forgotten we are awaited by the dear lady's dresser?"

Alicia had, in truth, forgotten that very thing, perhaps because she did not relish having her hair cut. Nevertheless she resolutely followed her aunt, trusting that a patroness of Almack's would not send an untalented wench who might ruin her lovely tresses.

Such trust was not misplaced, for the dresser was excellent and accomplished her task quickly, shortening the hair only around m'lady's youthful face and allowing it to remain long in the back. Both ladies were pleased with the results and exuberantly congratulated the dresser on her expertise, endearing themselves to the woman to such an extent that she almost refused the rather substantial remuneration they offered her.

It was left for Alicia to extol the woman's praises in a note to Lady Castlereagh, carried by the dresser as she returned to her mistress. Alicia also included in the note an expression of her sincere appreciation for the help which had been supplied at a time when her own error in judgment might have proven disastrous.

The afternoon was spent resting, since both ladies were tired from the strain of the previous night. Alicia slept overlong and was forced to dress quickly to avoid being late.

She had chosen to attend the costume ball as Helen of Troy, wearing a soft, thin—to the point of near-transparency—white tunic draped gently at the neck and caught at each shoulder with small gold clasps, then allowed to fall open, revealing long and graceful arms. A slender golden rope belted her, then crossed the bosom, artfully displaying her mature form. Greek style sandals were held on her dainty feet by leather thongs, crossed and tied above the ankle. Her hair was most becoming, framing her face with soft curls, the longer strands pulled up and back, then loosened to fall free in a cascade of gentle waves. A golden tiara crowned her head; a small golden armlet was her only other accessory. The total picture was strikingly beautiful in its simplicity, and Alicia smiled in satisfaction after taking one last glance in the mirror before catching up her mask and hurrying to join her aunt below.

As she descended the stairs, she could hear Sir Edmund's voice emanating from the drawing room. She was immediately reminded of her resolve to warn Aunt Matilda about her suspicions regarding that admittedly charming gentleman. It was too late to say anything now, she knew, and chided herself for being so forgetful. Tomorrow she simply had to have a serious discussion with her aunt.

The tiny hint of a frown she wore was replaced by a look of surprise when she entered the room and spied Sir Edmund. He was in costume, dressed as a French nobleman with a remarkable resemblance to King Louis XVI. The gentleman was going to the masquerade, and apparently he meant to accompany them.

Edmund turned at Alicia's entrance and slowly raised his quizzing glass, examining her with a detached air. He let it fall back on its golden chain after pronouncing her costume as quite striking. Before she could respond, however, his gaze returned to Matilda, who was smiling in a way that gave her face an inexplicable youthfulness. She stood resplendent in a magnificent gown of lavender satin trimmed with ivory lace. A high powdered wig topped the costume, clearly meant to portray the character of Marie Antoinette.

Alicia thanked him, greeting him politely even though she was unable to hide the fact that his presence was totally unexpected. In response to Sir Edmund's examination she walked around the couple, eyeing them carefully before complimenting them both on their choice of costume. Admittedly, the two made quite a handsome pair. She realized this must have been planned, and her suspicions of the man grew even more. She did not welcome an entire evening with him, and it showed in her voice. She could not repress the desire to send him a quick barb.

"How perfect you both look. One would never guess, Sir Edmund, that you chose to join us at the last moment."

"Oh, my dear," Matilda interrupted, "I would have told you sooner, but my memory failed me. So much has happened that it completely slipped my mind. You see, during that morning ride in the park when we became reacquainted after so many years, I mentioned the masquerade, thinking Sir Edmund might care to join us. Although he assured me at the time that such events were not to his liking, last evening he kindly offered to escort us, and I accepted gratefully. To have his protection at a costumed affair will be most advantageous." She beamed her approval, then glanced back at her niece with a slight frown of reproof. "I am persuaded that with such a revealing costume as yours, my dear, the presence of an escort is a necessity. Not expressing your appreciation does him a disservice."

Alicia, even more suspicious of the man after Matilda's explanation, but fearing her aunt might seriously consider canceling the evening's entertainment if she did not suppress her misgivings and exhibit at least a modicum of enthusiasm for Sir Edmund's company, quickly agreed and thanked the gentleman for his thoughtfulness. She would speak with Matilda in the morning. Tonight she would enjoy herself despite the discomfort of an unexpected escort.

Upon arriving at the ball, Alicia, feeling secure and anonymous behind her mask, soon became involved watching the costumed figures dance around the room. Flickering candles in flower-bedecked sconces lined the wall, and a huge crystal chandelier hung from the center of the room. The long doors that lined one side of the room were open, giving access to a balcony and stairs to the gardens below, which were charmingly decorated with oriental lanterns.

When a rather portly Henry VIII claimed her for a dance, she turned to her aunt for permission. Lady Matilda smiled her assent, then turned and accepted a dance with Sir Edmund. Alicia curtsied low to her partner, allowing herself to be caught up in the spirit of the evening.

"I am honored, Your Majesty," she said, smiling mischievously as she accepted his hand. "But pray, sire, do not treat me as poor Anne, for I have already lost my head, having gazed upon your glorious raiment."

" 'Tis I who have lost his head at your beauty," the costumed king replied gallantly before leading her onto the floor.

How exciting it was to dance with costumed strangers, to play a part, speaking from behind a mask, remaining mysterious and unrecognized. How easy it was to find the courage to flirt outrageously, reveling in her anonymity. Soon she felt happy and carefree, bubbling with tinkling laughter.

In a short space of time Alicia found herself partnered by a Roman tribune, two Louis XVIs—neither of whom carried off his role half so well as did Sir Edmund—and a devil who tried to act his part by holding her more closely to him than was deemed proper. She gave him a quick set-down, informing him that she would leave him standing alone on the dance floor looking perfectly ridiculous if he did not follow certain proprieties. He smiled ruefully and agreed, finishing the set in a much subdued fashion.

As she moved around the room, Alicia began to notice a tall figure standing to one side, unmoving, and, so she thought, watching her intently. He was dressed as a Cavalier, in full breeches and jerkin over a long-sleeved shirt, with wide cuffs and a large falling lace collar. His head was covered with a wide-brimmed hat trimmed with feathers. Bucket-top boots completed the picture admirably.

He wore a demi-mask, as did Alicia, and often her gaze was drawn unconsciously back to the stranger. Finally, when she had glanced toward him once too often, he removed his hat in a sweeping arc and made a most gallant bow. She colored deeply in embarrassment and turned away, vowing to refrain from looking again at a creature so presumptuous as to acknowledge her interest in him.

Such resolve was soon forgotten, however, and she glanced once more in his direction. Disappointment stung her as she realized he was gone. Without a thought to her partner, she turned her head about, searching the room for his presence. Suddenly she spied a figure standing in a shadowed corner, and without further investigation, knew for a certainty it was her Cavalier. A tingling sensation stabbed through her as she realized their gaze had met, even though she could not see his face. An invisible bond seemed to have formed, and she was powerless to resist it.

The set ended, and she mumbled her appreciation to her masked partner, accepting his offer of refreshment as she stood beside her aunt at the far end of the room. Soon a number of young gallants surrounded her, each pleading for her hand in the next dance. She remained silent, however, for as the music began again, her Cavalier stepped out of the shadows and walked toward her.

Shocked by her own boldness, she nevertheless dismissed the gentlemen with a wave of her delicate hand. "Forgive me, gentle sirs, but this dance has already been promised," she explained softly, then turned back, her breathing quite rapid and her pulse pounding, to watch the dashing figure approach.

He must be nobly born, she thought, watching the mysterious Cavalier closely, for he carried himself with an air of authority she felt to be nearly impossible to imitate by those of lesser birth. That he was dangerous she knew instinctively, but made no protest as he stood before her in silence. He offered his arm, which she accepted readily, a small smile quivering on her lips.

He placed his hand on her waist. She tingled at his touch. His piercing blue eyes, visible behind his mask, held her gaze steadfastly as they began to move to the strains of her favorite dance, the waltz. Trying to retain some control of the situation, she held herself stiffly at first, keeping a great deal of distance between them. Her body betrayed her, however, as it moved gracefully to the glorious music, in perfect unison with her partner, and her air of formality slipped away.

Slowly she surrendered to the magic that encompassed them and allowed herself to be drawn closer in a pleasant, but most improper position. Her knees were weak and her breathing strangely difficult as she trustingly followed his lead, responding to the slightest pressure of his hand.

She gasped as his lips, in an apparent accident, brushed against her temple, evoking a most pleasurable sensation which coursed through her body and ended at her toes. Such reactions were definitely not those of a well-bred young lady, she inwardly chided herself, but she continued to dance with him, remaining helpless in the grip of the new sensation, her body exquisitely aware of her partner's every movement.

They danced in silence, twirling about the room at a dizzying pace. When the music died, he guided her off the floor to the safekeeping of her aunt, and with another gallant bow, silently left her standing, eyes glistening, face flushed, and her mouth open in amazement.

Her hands trembled as she reached out for support, clutching at a fluted column topped by the bust of Augustus, which stood conveniently at her side. At Matilda's concerned gaze, she murmured a need for fresh air. With quivering limbs she slowly made her way to an open door, welcoming the draught of cool air that washed over her as she sank thankfully into the confines of an unoccupied chair.

A gnawing emptiness grew within her, a void that had previously gone totally unrecognized. She fought against it and the accompanying disappointment which had swept over her as the mysterious Cavalier abruptly withdrew his disturbing presence. In some inexplicable manner during that magical waltz, he had become important to her as no other man had ever been.

"Are you ill, my dear?" Lady Matilda asked, surprised to find her niece sitting alone. "I do hope you are not becoming feverish," she continued, her voice full of concern as she examined Alicia closely, noting the pale face relieved by two bright spots of color on her cheeks, and the overbright, glistening eyes. "Perhaps we should leave," she suggested.

"Oh, no. Do please stay a while longer," Alicia implored, anxious to dissuade her aunt. "I feel perfectly well now. It does seem rather close tonight, don't you agree?"

Matilda nodded in answer, her puzzled expression well hidden by her mask as she scrutinized the costumed figures milling about. "Very well, dear, we shall remain a short time longer, but I think we should still withdraw before the unmasking. I fear many in this company are sadly lacking in proper conduct, and their behavior promises to become even more unseemly as the evening progresses."

Alicia nodded, blushing slightly as she recalled her own actions a short time before. Inward restitution was made as she vowed to keep herself under strict control the remainder of the evening.

Matilda kept a watchful eye over her niece and began to relax as the young girl's color returned to normal. Soon Alicia was again surrounded by her admirers. Many offered to partner the entrancing Greek vision—as she was being called by the youngbloods that evening—but Alicia refused to take the floor again, preferring to put the moment to good use and practice quick repartee while she remained behind the costume and mask of Helen of Troy.

Again a waltz was played, and Alicia, recognizing the music, looked up expectantly, as if hoping to see her Cavalier. When his dashing figure did indeed appear again, she gasped in astonishment, shivering slightly with pleasure and anticipation. Again he silently offered his arm, which she accepted readily, leaving her admirers gaping as she left.

"Have you been away fighting the roundheads, sir?" she queried in a soft, silvery voice, attempting to bring lightness to this, their second meeting. "You *are* dedicated to King Charles, are you not?" she asked, beginning to doubt her knowledge of history in the face of his continued silence.

At long last he spoke, nodding slowly. " 'Tis my duty as a Royalist, pledged to the service of the Crown, but I shall cast it all away to do your bidding, oh queen of my heart." He too spoke in a light manner, but his deep voice held a strange note of sincerity.

"Ah, but I am queen no longer," she countered in mock sadness. "Helen of Troy gave up her throne for the love of Paris."

"Ah, yes. Paris gave Aphrodite the golden apple to gain the most beautiful woman in the world. But I am not Paris, and you are not Helen of Troy."

Alicia was startled for a moment. Her fantasy world began to crumble as his pronouncement called her back to reality. Fortunately she did not break in and take him to task, for his next words restored her to the wonderland the masquerade had helped to create.

"No," he whispered. "You cannot be Helen. Not a mere mortal. Rather a goddess—Aphrodite herself. And I am powerless in your presence," he added, huskily.

She shivered slightly at his words, thrilling to the romanticism just expressed, but believing his words were better applied to herself. She appeared to be the one who was powerless. His mere presence produced a severe constriction in her bosom, making breathing extremely difficult, yet inexplicably the sensation was most pleasant.

She was exquisitely aware of his masculine strength and grace as he spun her around the room. The magic enfolded her again, and she surrendered to it, leaning against him slightly, fearing she would fall without his support. There was no explanation for this stranger's effect upon her emotions, but it was most definitely real, and she ceased struggling against it. In truth, she dearly wished the dance would never end.

Alas, the final note died away, and they slowly walked to the side of the room. Instead of leaving her abruptly, however, as he had done previously, the mysterious Cavalier led her out one of the open doors and down into the garden where colored lanterns flickered, increasing the atmosphere of unreality. He guided her to a secluded corner and stopped, turning to face her.

Her heart pounded within her bosom, and a small shiver of fear sliced through her as she looked up at the masked face. Danger! she thought. Run! But she didn't. She couldn't.

He gripped her shoulders as if to keep her from running away. "You feel it too, don't you?" he whispered. "The magic. Our souls calling to each other, drawing near, blending. I know you feel the same. You must. Tell me you do."

She swallowed hard, then nodded shyly. She couldn't speak. Amazement filled her that he would speak of the strange magic she experienced.

"May I?" he asked quietly, slowly lifting his hand to her face. When she made no protest, he gently removed her mask. She heard a soft hiss of indrawn breath as he looked at her closely in the dim light. "You *are* a goddess," he whispered in adoration. "My golden Aphrodite."

She was paralyzed, unable to move or even cry out in protest as he slowly drew her to him, bending his head over hers. His kiss was gentle, his lips touching hers tenderly, and she quivered in his arms like a delicate bird. A pleasant sensation of warmth enveloped her. Again her limbs became strangely weak, and she once more surrendered to his strength, her lips parting slightly as she relaxed.

With a strange moan which seemed to be ripped from his inner being, he clasped her tightly and covered her entire mouth with his, seeming to draw her breath, her very soul to merge with his. Her head was swimming, and she felt herself sinking into a delicious darkness. She heard another moan, only vaguely aware that it had escaped from her own throat.

Suddenly she was free, gulping air gladly, yet strangely yearning to once again be the prisoner of his lips, to feel herself floating in warmth once more as a strange new sensation rose within her. Gently, trustingly, she leaned her head on his chest. She sensed, with inner conviction, that this was the emotion she had been missing in her young life. This was the glory about which she had heard and for which she had longed.

"Oh, my sweet, my golden Aphrodite," her Cavalier

whispered huskily in her ear. "I've searched for you my entire life. You've been a vision, the queen of my dreams. Now that I've found you, I'll never let you go." The movement of his lips against her ear sent delicious tingles down her arms, and she shivered slightly.

"Are you cold, my goddess?" he asked and smiled as she shook her head in a dazed fashion.

Her small, white hand reached up to touch his mask. "May I?" she finally whispered in a soft repetition of his earlier words.

"Allow me," he countered, freeing her for a moment to remove the stiffened cloth.

With a shy smile, Alicia looked up to see the face of her dashing gallant. One glance, however, was enough to bring a startled exclamation to her lips.

"Oh no!" she gasped. With strength suddenly returning to her limbs, she pushed the astonished Cavalier away and ran blindly toward the house. Her Cavalier, the gentleman she had allowed to kiss her, was none other than the detestable, the odious Marquess of Brodhurst!

# = 7 =

LORD BRODHURST STOOD PARALYZED for a moment, watching his goddess disappear into the crowd of masked figures. Her unexpected recoil upon unmasking him had left him dumbfounded, but he quickly struggled to regain his composure. He could not lose her. Not now, when he had just found the woman of his dreams. He ran after the fleeing figure, searching frantically among the dancers, but he was too late. She had vanished.

Why had she run away? What had frightened her? It must have been his boorish behavior. He had kissed her. In defense of his actions, however, he had to acknowledge that the kiss had arisen naturally after gazing at such a vision of loveliness so gloriously revealed upon removal of her mask. Had she but given protest, he might have resisted those inner urgings. But no, she seemed willing, even responsive, to his touch. As he mulled over the problem, he finally came upon an acceptable solution. The beauty must have run from him in confusion upon realizing she had allowed him untoward liberties. A well-bred young lady could have done no less under the circumstances. She had not fled from him, but rather from her own injudicious conduct. That was it. Now he had only to find her. But where? She would undoubtedly leave the ball immediately.

There being no answer forthcoming, he slowly made his way through the crowd of glittering, costumed revelers toward the stairs. Once enclosed in his town carriage, he leaned back against the soft red velvet cushion and closed his eyes, remembering vividly the events of the evening.

He had decided to attend the masquerade only after Sir Edmund had implied he was planning to go—no small matter since that gentleman had often proclaimed his dislike of such affairs, calling them foolish or even juvenile activities.

That something, or more likely someone, had enough influence to cause the appearance of his friend at a costume ball was enough to pique Brodhurst's curiosity. He also had been in the doldrums, having made no discernible progress in the problem of his unwanted betrothal, and decided a masquerade might be the very thing to lift his spirits.

At the ball, however, he soon relinquished all thought of finding Edmund. For in a short space of time he had already encountered three individuals dressed as King Louis, none of whom proved to be his friend. As he lounged against the wall, content to watch the parade of costumes before him, his eye was inescapably drawn to the figure of a young lady in gold and white who had just entered the room. Her gown was strikingly simple, clinging softly to her limbs, displaying her charms in a delicate manner.

He watched as she seemed to float around the room, carrying herself proudly as if she were, in reality, a queen. His ears could faintly detect her tinkling laughter, even when her form was hidden from his view by the crush of guests in the ballroom.

Unable to tear his eyes away from her, he was not surprised to find she noticed his stare. Her resulting interest in him, however, was unexpected. She did not flirt. Rather she simply appeared to respond to an invisible bond which began developing between them.

He fought against his rising interest. Females were always a distinct problem to him—well-bred ones, that is—for he was well versed in the handling of birds of paradise. The problem was that as long as he could remember, it seemed he carried a mental vision of the woman he would love and marry. Each lady who drew his eye was unconsciously compared to this concept of perfection, and it was understandable that they all failed miserably.

He did not want to be disappointed again. Nevertheless wisdom lost the battle, and he pushed aside all misgivings. In an effort to observe this walking dream appearing before him as Helen of Troy in an undisturbed fashion, he found a darkened corner and contented himself to watching her grace of movement while remaining unseen himself. His shock at being detected by the object of his attention was understandably immense.

She could not possibly have seen him—on that point he was certain—looking as she had from a position of brightness under the huge chandelier into the dimness of his corner. No, it was not ordinary vision but something greater, as if their souls had reached out to each other—touched, and gloried in recognition. He had been inexplicably filled with a great joy.

Without considering the consequences, he went to her silently, dazed, unable to resist longer the temptation to touch a dream. Miraculously she responded, slipping into his arms without speaking as though understanding his need for silence, his desire to keep the illusion which her voice might dispel of having finally found his ideal woman.

As they danced, he detected the faint aroma of violets from her hair, a pure, delicate scent, far superior in his estimation to some of the cloying perfumes other women had used in an effort to arouse his desire. Slowly a feeling of tenderness and protectiveness filled him as his lady relaxed, leaning slightly on him for support.

At the end of the dance he was so inwardly shaken as to be unable to utter a single word. There was nothing for him to do but turn and leave. At that moment it had been his intent to quit the masquerade, to enjoy in privacy the short-lived pleasure this illusion of having met his soulmate would bring. The temptation, however, to test this dream come true was too great, and once again he approached the lovely Greek vision.

She spoke this time in pure, sweet tones, lightly quizzing him on his costume. He had tried to identify the lady, a task of no little difficulty, and he had hoped her voice would give him some clue. But though it sounded vaguely familiar, he could match it to no face other than the one which had often filled his dreams. Yes, it was exactly the voice his vision of perfection should have.

It was inevitable that he should seek the final test, entertaining little hope that the illusion would prove to be a reality. The unmasking was a moment of magic. He looked into huge blue eyes filled with trust, innocence, and a slight hint of fear. Soft wisps of hair lay in gentle curls against her temples, moist from the exertion of their waltz. Her skin was translucent, as delicate and fine in texture as a child's. A tiny nose, ever so slightly upturned, was a perfect companion to the small, delicate mouth.

He caught his breath. She was beautiful! Here was the goddess who had ruled his dreams. At last, he had found her. The familiar face of his ideal woman had leapt from the illusive fantasies of his mind to become reality, to stand before him in the flickering light of the garden.

The kiss which followed was inevitable. At first he touched her lips tentatively, fearing the dream would evaporate. To his great relief she proved real. Her delicate response was too much for his overburdened self-control, and suddenly all his frustration, desire, and joy were unleashed, and he crushed her in his arms as if in one kiss he hoped to merge their lives forever.

Finally regaining some of his senses, he released her, surprised to find his goddess still leaning against him, unprotesting. He whispered in her ear, vowing never to let her go, wondering if she understood the intensity in his voice. Then, removing his own mask, he had watched her expression change from shy expectancy to one of shock and revulsion. She had then pushed herself free and run as if he were the devil incarnate.

Brodhurst wiped away the perspiration that had formed on his brow as he relived the agony of his loss. Again he pondered the reason for her flight and realized he no longer could delude himself that it was the kiss that had caused her to flee. There was only one possible conclusion.

"She recognized me," he muttered into the darkness of his carriage. "By God, my sins have come to roost!" He pounded his fist against the carriage door in exasperation.

"Be ye wanting to stop, m'lord?" the driver hollered down as he pulled in the smartly stepping pair of matched bays in response to his lordship's pounding.

"No. Drive on," the marquess ordered. He settled back once more, mindful not to express himself so violently if he wished to continue his contemplation undisturbed.

Leaning his head against his hand, Brodhurst reviewed his life, regretting the selfish, egotistical, and often high-handed manner he had treated the ladies of his acquaintance. His reputation must have driven the girl away. Well, he would amend his life, prove his worth, and win her hand.

First, however, he had to find her, and he had not the slightest inkling whatsoever of her name. Also, of course, there was the matter of that detestable marriage agreement. He vowed to see the Lady Alicia as soon as possible and convince her to release him. There would be no more tricks, no more frustrations. He would ask her forthrightly and pay whatever she required if necessary, but he would gain his freedom. To that intent he pledged his entire being.

Alicia spent a restless night, her mind beset with confusing memories. She recalled the sneering face of Lord Brodhurst as he looked down at her in disgust only a few weeks earlier, accusing her of duplicity and fraud. She could still hear his voice etching her with the acid of each quietly spoken word. She despised him for all the pain he had caused her. Yet, at the masquerade, she had willingly kissed him.

Admittedly, she had no knowledge of his identity at the time, but it was galling to think she had been so deeply affected by the odious marquess. Her memory of a dashing Cavalier was still vivid, and a strange sensation, not wholly unpleasant, tingled through her each time she recalled how he had bent and captured her lips.

"Ridiculous," she muttered in the silence of her room, as if by speaking aloud she might still the frantic workings of her confused mind. Peace was denied her, however. Mental visions of two faces floated before her: one smiling softly, the other sneering. That both countenances belonged to the same gentleman was nearly impossible for her to comprehend. At intervals she was cast into the depths of humiliation with the realization that she had embraced a known rake, the very individual who had caused her such anguish during her first Season, and the gentleman who had had the abominable gall to accuse her of being a fortune hunter.

She would then be rescued from her sense of shame and her spirits raised by the comforting thought that the gentleman who had affected her so strangely, called her his golden Aphrodite, and held her gently while vowing never to let her go, could not possibly be totally vile. Perhaps she had misjudged him.

Thus, she tossed in bed, her body reflecting the inability of her mind to find rest. Finally, in the predawn grayness, she ceased to struggle further. Acknowledging that sleep was impossible, she rose and began to dress.

Mary answered the unexpectedly early summons yawning prodigiously, a fact which gave her mistress a momentary twinge of guilt and caused the lady to make an inward promise to reward the girl at a later time.

Deciding an early morning ride might clear her head, Alicia sent word to the stables for Thomas to bring the horses round and accompany her to Hyde Park. Then, with Mary's help, she donned her favorite blue velvet riding habit, thankful for its comforting warmth as she did so.

Shortly after dawn, she and Thomas turned their

horses onto Park Lane and trotted briskly toward Rotten Row. The crisp early morning air was refreshing, making Alicia come near regretting having worn her heavy veil. The hour was early, and the cloud cover appeared thick enough to protect her delicate complexion. Unfortunately the dark circles under her eyes were mute testimony to her troubled night and must needs be hidden in case she encountered some other early riser. Finding reasons for her condition acceptable to curious and inquiring acquaintances would no doubt be difficult. The presence of the veil, however, eliminated any such problem.

The park appeared deserted, just as Alicia had expected, and the urge which had been with her since the first moment she had decided on such an early morning excursion finally took charge. She cast aside all sense of propriety and loosened her hold on the reins, giving Starfire her head. The feisty roan immediately surged forward into a full run, swiftly leaving Thomas far behind. Both horse and rider seemed to glory in the exercise. Alicia, well aware that such a sprint was highly improper for a well-bred lady of the ton, felt the risk involved in being detected was far outweighed by the freedom and joy she experienced on the back of her beloved Starfire.

All good things must needs end, and Alicia finally pulled up, slowing to a dignified walk before turning back to rejoin her groom. To be seen riding at such a breakneck pace was certainly risking censure, but to be observed riding without escort was nearly unforgivable.

Fortunately she had reached Thomas just before the silhouette of a solitary rider became dimly visible farther down the path. Unaccountably irritated at the appearance of an intruder into her privacy, she started off at a lively trot, intending to pass the rider with an air of haste to avoid being stopped and drawn into any long and tedious conversation in the event she and the rider were acquainted. Although she soon remembered that her veil would render her unrecognizable to most everyone she might meet, she refrained from slackening her pace.

As the distance between the riders diminished, a distinct sinking sensation gripped the lady, for she recognized the gentleman approaching as none other than the very person who had caused her such mental distress and lack of sleep and thus the principal reason for her early visit to the park. To meet the marquess was unthinkable, yet there appeared to be no possibility of avoiding just such an occurrence, for although she did not slow her horse, his lordship turned, caught up with her, and matched her speed perfectly, obviously desiring to converse with her.

"Lady Alicia, it must be you," he stated in a tone of strained politeness. "There can be no other who hides her features so thoroughly."

Her heartbeat quickened and her throat constricted to such an extent she could not answer, only nod her head in acknowledgment.

"We meet by chance, but perhaps it is for the best. My intention is to call upon you today. Perhaps you can advise me of the most opportune time. I must discuss a matter with your father."

Without slackening her pace, Alicia shook her head, swallowed, and forced herself to speak. "The earl still resides in the country. You have a long ride if you desire to speak with him." She turned toward him in curiosity. "Pray, tell me, what you could possibly have to discuss with my father. Could it perhaps concern me?"

"You know it must," he replied.

Once again her heartbeat quickened. "Then discuss it with me and no other," she demanded, "and since fate has seen fit to have us meet so early in the morning, let us not put off until later what can be accomplished now."

"As you wish, my lady," he replied. "May I request that you slow to a pace more conducive to conversation, for the matter I have to discuss is of importance to us both." His tone was not the usual sarcastic one Alicia had come to associate with the marquess, and, unable to deny such a reasonable request, she slowed her mount to a more leisurely walk.

"Is this more to your liking, sir?" she asked, her voice high and strained. "Or would you prefer we dismount and walk?"

A slight quiver at the corner of his mouth finally spread into a faint smile as Brodhurst considered the deplorable state of the Row that morning. Walking was definitely out of the question. He acknowledged a certain appreciation for her wry humor. "No, this is quite acceptable, my lady." He paused for a moment as if gathering strength for his next utterance, then cleared his throat and began in a most formal manner.

"My dear Lady Alicia, ours has certainly not been a warm and friendly relationship, to be sure." He paused, clearing his throat once more. "Perhaps my own attitude and actions have contributed to this less than enjoyable situation. If so, then I beg your forgiveness." The pained expression which passed over his features as he pronounced those words would normally have brought a giggle from Alicia's lips, had she not been shocked into silence as she realized he was actually offering her an apology. Again she could only nod in acknowledgment.

"My lady, although we are bound by a marriage agreement, I'm certain that we would not suit. Therefore, I respectfully request that you release me from the contract." He paused after this formal declaration, obviously waiting for Alicia to respond.

"I thought we had already discussed this at an earlier meeting," Alicia replied, relieved that this time her voice was pitched only a modicum higher than normal. "At that time I do believe I expressed my reluctance to dissolve our agreement, did I not?"

"True. You gave me no doubt as to your intentions in this regard. But I cannot believe that you truly wish to become my wife, and most certainly I have no desire to be your husband!"

"Oh?" Alicia responded haughtily, her pride helping to overcome her anxiety. "And why do you choose to point this out to me again at this time?"

"A matter has arisen which makes it essential for me

to find an immediate and satisfactory solution to this unfortunate situation."

Alicia found her thoughts so confused as to render her momentarily speechless. She urged her horse into a trot, hoping to give herself a few moments before Lord Brodhurst could catch up with her. His manner was quite civil, and she inwardly approved of his direct approach. Yet she was strangely reluctant to free him, even though her original plan to obtain revenge had essentially been abandoned.

He quickly drew level with her again, and she once again slowed to a leisurely walk, effectively placing herself behind him and forcing him to rein in the perplexed animal beneath him. She smiled at his mumbled expletive. When they were once again abreast, her silence seemed to prod him further.

"My lady, again I ask you to please reconsider. If money is of such prime importance, rest assured I am prepared to meet with your father and pay any suitable financial penalty. Let us be done with this matter. Name your price."

Stung by his mention of money, Alicia emerged from her bemused state and considered his words in the light of their meeting some weeks earlier. Clearly, he still considered her a fortune hunter, a lady so lacking in character or principle that she could be bought off with a few paltry guineas. Memories of Matilda's comments concerning the Brodhurst fortune came to mind, and she found her voice in retort.

"Sir, if my memory serves me well, it is my opinion that financial considerations were part of the agreement. I may have been misinformed, however, for I was led to believe that it was you who expected to benefit from the alliance. A matter of my inheritance, I understand."

Lord Brodhurst's eyes widened at her counterattack, then he nodded ever so slightly, acknowledging the accuracy of her verbal barb.

"And since you were looking to increase your holdings upon our marriage," Alicia continued, "how does it happen, my lord, that you are now prepared to pay for the dissolution of our contract?" Her voice was strained, sounding almost foreign to her own ears, and she held herself stiffly erect as she questioned his lordship.

He, too, seemed to be experiencing a certain amount of discomfort, for he rode without his usual easy grace. He did not immediately respond to Alicia's question, staring forward as if in deep concentration. He cleared his throat once again and began speaking slowly, choosing each word carefully.

"I don't expect you to understand," he said quietly. "Last night I met—" Unable to find appropriate words, he squared his shoulders and lifted his chin as his voice took on a clear, determined tone. "I have already made it quite clear that I have no inclination to marry you. Now I wish the entire matter dropped and the cloud over my future cleared away."

*Last night.* The words flashed through her mind. His change of attitude has something to do with last night. Her heart seemed to skip a beat. She was strangely pleased, but although such emotion should normally have inclined her to grant his request and put an end to the charade, she was as yet unable to bring herself to the point of releasing him.

"I will give due consideration to your words, sir," she replied formally, her voice again sounding a trifle high and somewhat strained. "You will be informed of my decision. Good day, my lord." With those crisp words she urged Starfire into a brisk trot and, thankful for the veil which hid her flushed cheeks, quickly left the marquess to his own company.

Once back at Wynford House, Alicia fled to her room, giving orders not to be disturbed. After stepping out of her habit, she crawled into the welcome softness of her bed, quickly falling into a deep and restful sleep, a soft smile of contentment on her lips.

Lord Brodhurst had watched Alicia and her groom disappear down the Row, then stroked his chin thoughtfully before turning his horse and resuming his morning ride. The exercise did not hold its usual pleasure for him, and soon he headed back to his own house. After a late breakfast, a strange restlessness overtook the marquess, one which prodded him into a decision to see his man of business immediately. Rather than waste time waiting for the man to be summoned to Brodhurst House, he decided to drive to St. James himself.

Mr. Craighton was surprised to see his lordship, but ushered him cordially into his office. The gentlemen spoke at length about finances, and Brodhurst was pleased to discover his situation much improved. Some timely investments and skillful managing had combined to bring the estate around, providing an excess available for improvements to his holdings which the marquess had always wanted to make. Once the initial pleasure had worn off, however, the thought that he must buy his way out of that odious marriage agreement quickly sobered the young gentleman. He told Craighton of his intention to offer the earl money for his release, and was assured that formal papers could be drawn up immediately by a solicitor so that when the transaction was made his lordship would no longer be under any obligation whatsoever to the family.

Brodhurst left the office looking somewhat reserved. His unusual contemplative mood caused immediate comment from acquaintances as he entered White's, for instead of acknowledging and joining those friends who called to him, as was his wont, he took a seat in the corner, staring out the window with eyes clouded in thought.

"Considering joining the Bow Window Set, Jonathan?" a friendly, hearty voice broke into his reverie.

The marquess looked up to see who would intrude on his contemplations, eyes full of sparks and tongue prepared to unleash a telling set-down. Immediately upon identifying the intruder, however, he relaxed, his features softening into a smile of welcome.

"Edmund, my friend. Good to see you. Join me,

please." As the older gentleman moved to draw a chair close and settle himself, Brodhurst continued, "I attended the masquerade last night."

"Did you now?" Edmund commented, surprised.

"Yes. Found an old costume I hadn't worn for quite some time, and decided to try the water, so to speak, especially since you had already announced your intention of doing the same. Looked for you, but no luck. Tell me honestly, did you actually attire yourself as Louis XVI and attend?"

"Most certainly," Edmund replied indignantly, drawing himself up to a stiffly erect position, prepared to counter any attempt at ridicule by his friend. "Escorted the Lady Alicia and her aunt, just as I intended. Didn't you believe me?"

"Yes, of course," the younger man was quick to soothe his friend's feelings. "But knowing your past attitude toward such festivities, I merely wondered if perhaps you had second thoughts about the matter and had withdrawn."

"Certainly not," Sir Edmund replied, his voice slightly tinged with rebuke. "A Coswell does not back down from a commitment."

Brodhurst nodded, acknowledging the truth of that statement. "Of course. My apologies. The thought should never have entered my mind." He hesitated, then continued with a sympathetic voice. "Such a friend you are, Edmund, to go to these lengths just because you promised to keep a close eye on that household for me." He clasped the gentleman by the shoulder. "I am fortunate, indeed, to have you as a comrade. Your sacrifice on my behalf will never be forgotten."

Sir Edmund, completely mollified, relaxed noticeably. "Couldn't exactly call it a sacrifice," he replied with slight embarrassment. "Enjoyed myself, actually." He hesitated, gazing abstractedly at some distant point, a strange smile on his lips. "A fine woman, Brodhurst. Witty, charming, and blessed with a kind and gentle nature."

Lord Brodhurst appeared startled by his friend's

words. "Are you serious?" he asked, aware that the gentleman had never before spoken in such a manner regarding a female, at least not that he could recollect during the many years that they had been close friends. He continued, "But surely you have not forgotten her financial condition?" He refrained from mentioning the young lady's features, knowing that his friend, once impressed by a person's inner nature, had little regard for outward appearances, a trait, he acknowledged, which was sadly lacking in his own character.

"Humph!" Sir Edmund snorted. "Don't care a whit about money. Have plenty of my own, you know. Breeding's the thing, however, and she comes from a fine line. Think perhaps you've misjudged the family, my boy."

Brodhurst, certain that his friend was near to being trapped in the web of that unscrupulous woman, was preparing to argue the point when he became aware of the presence of a young gentleman at his side.

Geoffrey Baugh stood stiffly, hesitant to interrupt two such notable gentlemen, yet firm in his desire to speak. When his presence was acknowledged, he bowed formally.

"Beg pardon for interrupting, but I simply must express my deep appreciation for your sponsorship. Words can't describe what membership at White's means to me. I had intended to thank you individually, but finding you both together was an opportunity impossible to disregard. I am in your debt, gentlemen." He bowed slightly once more, and muttering his thanks again, prepared to take his leave, plainly grateful for having had the opportunity to relieve himself of such a burden.

"One moment," Brodhurst called out gently, clearly impressed by the young gentleman's sincere words and respectful demeanor, and feeling not a little guilt at his own plans for using Geoffrey to help him escape Lady Alicia's clutches. "Come, join us. Tell us of your first impressions of this famous Tory stronghold."

Geoffrey, brightening at the invitation, immediately complied. He proceeded to chat amicably, discussing the few members he had already met and stating his conviction that nowhere could he find himself in better company than at White's. His pride was quite apparent, and his two sponsors smiled indulgently.

"Have you seen Lady Alicia lately?" the marquess asked, unable to control his curiosity further.

"Oh yes, I'm a frequent visitor, as Sir Edmund can attest." He smiled conspiratorially at the older gentleman, then looked back at Brodhurst. "Our paths have often met in that household."

This added information regarding his friend's involvement with the family gave Brodhurst cause to reflect. Was Sir Edmund in imminent danger of being ensnared in a trap similar to the one in which he had found himself? Such a thing must not be allowed to happen. He was pondering the problem when young Geoffrey's voice broke his train of thought.

"The Lady Alicia is perfection," he said devotedly. "No other woman can compare with such an angel. I consider myself honored to be counted among her friends."

"Appears to me as if you aspire to much more than friendship," Brodhurst said, glancing toward his friend to notice that gentleman's reaction to his statement. But Sir Edmund merely sat quietly, surveying the new member with his cool gray eyes partially hooded.

"Oh no, sir . . . I mean yes, sir . . . uh . . . I mean yes, I would aspire to make her my very own, but I am unworthy. She would not have me."

Such sentiments captured Brodhurst's attention. Perhaps there was still a possibility of freeing himself from that unwanted betrothal without the necessity of plundering his newfound monetary surplus. "Have you asked her?" he queried.

"Oh, no!" the young gentleman exclaimed, plainly embarrassed by the turn this conversation had taken. "I thought only to nourish our friendship, hoping that someday her feelings for me might deepen. If such an event occurred, naturally I would first approach her father."

"Balderdash!" the marquess snorted. "If you want the

lady, go after her. Courage, man. It is a poorly kept secret that my great-grandfather carried off the bride of his choice. She had nothing to say in the matter. They were quite happy together, so I have been told." He cordially slapped Geoffrey on the back. "Take heart, my boy. Press your attentions. Perhaps you can fix her interest. Are you seeing her soon?"

"This evening, actually," Geoffrey answered. "I have the honor of escorting the ladies to Almack's."

"Almack's!" Brodhurst exclaimed with incredulity, wondering how Alicia had managed to obtain vouchers.

"Lady Matilda has a friendship of long standing with Lady Castlereagh, I believe," Sir Edmund interjected, answering the unspoken question on his friend's face.

"That explains it," the marquess said, nodding in understanding.

"Plan to attend myself," Edmund continued. "Haven't been there for years."

This last statement worried the marquess even more, for he had no doubt about the identity of the magnet which drew his friend to the assembly rooms that evening.

"Care to join me?" Edmund asked. "Every eligible female, acceptable in the highest circles of the ton, will be there. Perhaps you may find someone interesting."

Brodhurst, already of half a mind to follow suit, if only to protect his friend from Lady Alicia, recalled his intense desire to find the mysterious lady of his dreams who had disappeared the previous evening. That vision of loveliness might easily be among those attending the assembly. Without conscious decision, he accepted the offer.

Alicia awoke to the light sound of tapping on her bedroom door. Late afternoon sunlight streamed in through the window, illuminating the smiling face of Aunt Matilda as she peered in.

"Are you feeling all right, my dear?" she asked, concern evident in her voice. "I fear you have slept nearly the entire day away."

The young lady yawned and stretched languidly. "Oh

yes, Aunt Matilda, I'm feeling much better now. A little sleep was all I needed after two restless nights." She stretched again, a strange little smile playing at her lips.

"Oh," Matilda replied. "I had no idea your night was troubled. Have you a problem of which I'm unaware, dear?" The question was accompanied by a shrewd glance.

"No, no," Alicia responded quickly. "I'm persuaded it was just the excitement. My first masquerade, you know."

"I'm more inclined to believe you were just overtired. I have often experienced the problem myself. Strange, is it not, that at times when rest is needed most, it is nearly impossible to obtain until of necessity one drops from sheer exhaustion." Matilda smiled. "Of course, when one is young exhaustion is easily cured."

"Whatever the problem, dear aunt, it doesn't signify. I am certainly much improved now. A little weak, perhaps, but nothing a little nourishment won't correct. Have I missed tea?"

Matilda smiled broadly, quickly shaking her head. "I waited, dear, hoping perhaps you might join me. Shall I have it served in here?"

"No, I think not. I prefer to come down. Movement might serve to help me regain my strength more quickly. Just allow me a few moments to dress, please."

"Very well. I will have it served in a quarter hour, if that is agreeable." Matilda waited for her niece's nod of assent before turning to leave.

Alicia smiled at the thoughtfulness of her aunt. In truth she was feeling quite pleased about everything in general, a surprising state of mind considering the tension and anxiety she had experienced the past two days. She was at a loss to explain such peace of mind, but was content to accept it, refraining from searching for reason.

She summoned Mary and dressed quickly, foregoing a thorough toilette until later, when it would be time to prepare for Almack's. Almack's! The mere thought of that imposing assemblage of the haute ton would at one time have weakened her knees and sent her pulse racing in anxiety. Now, her pulse quickened but from excitement only. This time she looked forward to the evening, confident of her ability to converse and mingle easily in such an august gathering.

"I certainly have changed," she announced and walked out of the room, leaving Mary to ponder the meaning of her mistress's last remark.

Tea was rather short, with Lady Matilda doing most of the talking while Alicia ate as if famished. The return of her appetite brought a smile of approval from the older lady.

"I do hope you regain your strength, dear, for this evening may prove to be quite a strain. In truth, I am reconsidering the advisability of attending tonight. Wouldn't you prefer to rest at home?"

Alicia quickly swallowed the last bite of food she had taken and spoke in protest. "Oh no, Aunt Matilda, pray do not cry off on my account. I am feeling quite restored, truly I am."

"Very well, dear, we shall go. But I must have your promise to apprise me the very moment you feel even the slightest bit unwell." She waited until Alicia nodded her assent absentmindedly while pouring herself another cup of tea, then continued, "Let us hope you will find someone interesting tonight, for I am persuaded you are not content with Mr. Baugh."

At the mention of young Geoffrey's name, Alicia smiled gently. "How astute of you to notice. He is a good and faithful friend, but nothing more. I find myself wishing for more stimulating conversation, although I must admit he has a great deal of wit. I laugh often in his presence, but I certainly have not developed a *tendre* for him. Perhaps I do need a gentleman with a bit more dash."

"Yes, and perhaps one a few more years your senior," Matilda mused. "Maturity can make quite a difference. Most young gentlemen feel that we need no intellectual stimulation whatsoever and rely on a few compliments and words of devotion to bring us contentment."

"How shallow they must think us," Alicia said, shaking

her head sadly. "Unfortunately, I am of the opinion that in many instances they are quite correct."

"I fear you have the right of it, child—a fact which makes matters even more difficult. That is why I will feel the absence of Sir Edmund most keenly this evening. I fear I have come to rely on his companionship. Unfortunately, Almack's has held little interest for him in the past, and I am persuaded tonight will prove no exception."

Alicia, realizing her aunt had revealed a startling amount of interest in that particular gentleman, was surprisingly unaffected. She felt no alarm as Matilda spoke so approvingly of Sir Edmund. His presence no longer seemed menacing, and she agreed that he would be sorely missed. It was not surprising, however, that her thoughts soon switched to consideration of his friend, Lord Brodhurst. But, this time such contemplation evoked neither anger nor a sense of pain or humiliation. A strange smile played at her lips again as she finished her tea in silence.

# === 8 ===

ALICIA SMILED DOWN AT young Mr. Baugh, who stood waiting in the hall to greet the ladies who descended the stairs together. He fidgeted nervously with his lapel, cut in the stylish "M" made popular by the Beau himself.

Tonight, Alicia wore a gown of green taffeta with a double-layered overskirt of green and blue spider gauze. A multilayered gauze stole of the same two colors was artfully draped over her shoulders, and small clusters of diamonds and emeralds sparkled at her ears and around her neck. As she descended, the colors shifted, blending and then separating again, as if part of a deep and mysterious sea.

Matilda appeared younger than her years in a gown of coral sarsenet, her hair piled high in an elegant coiffure.

Geoffrey, unable to take his eyes from the vision approaching him, swallowed and attempted to loosen his collar somewhat. Lady Alicia was a lovely lady, he knew, but tonight she was magnificent, seeming to glow, to radiate from within. Her eyes glistened, and a soft smile curved her lips gently. There was a new air of depth about her, an impression of mystery which seemed to be enhanced by the changing colors of her gown. She was simply bewitching, he decided, fighting valiantly to refrain from being struck speechless as had happened on previous occasions.

As the ladies donned their capes and descended the front steps to the carriage he had hired for the evening,

Geoffrey quickly took a drink from the thin flask he had secreted in the pocket of his greatcoat. For this night's work, he decided, a great deal of fortification was needed, necessitating the drinking of something stronger than lemonade, the only beverage to be found served at Almack's.

He followed the ladies into the carriage and seated himself beside Lady Matilda. From this vantage, he could afford himself a delightful opportunity to contemplate to his heart's content the delicate line of his beloved's throat and the exquisite curve of her lips, unencumbered by rules of etiquette, for the darkness cloaked him and kept his companions from immediately discerning the direction of his gaze. The enormity of the undertaking he planned for later that evening again intruded upon his pleasant contemplation, bringing with it the temptation to once again partake of the contents of his flask and fortify his courage. Tonight could bring to fruition his one great hope and dream. Tonight the angel seated across from him could be his.

The small party arrived at the assembly rooms on King Street in good time and were greeted personally by Lady Castlereagh, an honor she seldom accorded anyone. This night, however, the renowned hostess was of the opinion that the ladies needed to be viewed as totally acceptable in order to offset any lingering doubt due to Alicia's remarkable waltz at the Hargraves' ball. In a surprising effort to ensure her success, Lady Castlereagh proceeded to introduce a distant connection, Baron Wycliff, to Alicia.

The tall, pleasant-faced gentleman was quick to grasp what he considered to be a golden opportunity and secured Alicia's hand for the next dance before Geoffrey could open his mouth. Soon the lovely lady was surrounded by young bucks vying for her attention, and she found herself almost constantly on the dance floor, chatting animatedly while executing the most intricate steps with ease.

Exhausted after a particularly exhilarating country dance, Alicia rested, sipping lemonade while listening to the baron, who had been singularly attentive, regale her with stories of the hunt and the Wycliff seat in Northumberland, a shared interest in horses having already been established earlier.

Belatedly coming to the realization she had not noticed Geoffrey or her aunt in quite some time, Alicia searched the crowd for a familiar face, relaxing visibly upon spying dear Aunt Matilda in an animated discussion with none other than Sir Edmund. Pleased that an enjoyable evening was now assured for her aunt, Alicia turned back and bestowed a brilliant smile on the baron, rendering that gentleman speechless for a moment in admiration, the second time within the space of only a few days that she had had such a devastating effect upon an admirer. To his credit the baron recovered himself quickly, however, and continued the conversation skillfully.

Alicia listened attentively, adding a few comments, which her companion judged to be most witty, and expressing amusement in appropriate moments. The baron's attentions were most gratifying, and she found herself enjoying his company until a peculiar sensation drew her attention away from the conversation. The back of her neck prickled, and she was overwhelmed suddenly by a sense of isolation. Voices in the room seemed muffled, and she had the distinct impression she was no longer a part of the festivities. The orchestra began a waltz, and the strange sensation of *déjà vu* filled her. She looked around slowly, completely ignoring a question put to her by the baron, and found herself staring directly into the eyes of the Marquess of Brodhurst, who stood at the entrance of the assembly room.

He reached her in no more than three strides, bent low over her hand, and then in true Cavalier fashion, led her onto the dance floor to join the waltz that was still forming, all this with not one word having been spoken between them.

Alicia, feeling as if she were caught in a dream, could do nothing but follow his lead. Her lips parted slightly in an inaudible gasp as his hand cupped her waist, sending delicious shivers up her back. She could not tear her gaze from his, for he looked down upon her with a soft, gentle smile as his eyes, traveling over her face, caressed it tenderly, astounding her by weaving such magic that she could almost feel their gentle touch physically.

He drew her hand to his lips, kissing the tips of her fingers gently, sending tingles up her arm as they swirled around the room. Realizing that he was making most improper advances toward her, she lowered her eyes in embarrassment and confusion for a moment. Under the eyes of all the ton he was making love to her, she thought wildly but was strangely unmoved to draw away from him. If truth be told, she struggled mightily against a shocking desire to lean even closer.

For a short moment only was she at a loss to understand her own emotions. Suddenly, however, the barriers of her mind crumbled and the answer stood revealed, nearly blinding in its clarity. She loved the marquess! She loved him and had held a *tendre* for the gentleman, unknowingly to be sure, for quite some time. With such an insight, the last vestiges of anxiety and tension left her being, and she relaxed visibly, her smile broadened and her gaze, full of adoration, met his boldly, evoking a light of admiration in his own eyes.

The couple twirled gracefully around the room, oblivious to the comments they evoked from every group they passed. Soon the entire room was buzzing about the marquess's marked attention to the Lady Alicia. Young ladies and their mamas, lashing out in envy and frustration, spoke about her want of conduct.

Lady Castlereagh, having noticed the marquess when he first entered the assembly, was surprised that he lacked his normal practiced air of indifference as his eyes searched the room. She had smiled knowingly as he made directly for the Lady Alicia, pleased that her intuition was about to be proven correct once again. The smile faded, and she became more and more agitated, however, as the couple circled the dance floor, for the marquess was holding his partner much closer than was deemed proper, and Alicia was leaning forward as if inviting a full embrace. The distraught hostess, to be truthful, had the distinct impression that such an occurrence was imminent.

Both Lady Jersey—"Silence" as she was known to her friends—and Lady Cowper had noticed the couple by this time and were frowning in disapproval. The whispers were not loud enough to reach the dancers, however, especially the couple whose total world, at least for the moment, existed only in each other's eyes.

The dance ended and the floor cleared, but Brodhurst and Alicia remained in the center of the room, isolated and unaware of the words of censure being spoken around them.

"Tonight I am blessed beyond all mortal men," the marquess said, breaking his silence, "for I dance with a goddess once again." He glanced down at her gown appreciatively, then returned his gaze to her glowing face. "This evening you are Aphrodite, rising from the waves."

Alicia, never thinking to bat her eyes or flirt lightheartedly in response to his compliment, as would most other girls of her acquaintance, merely smiled dreamily. Thinking, however, that perhaps some response was expected, she spoke softly in the same vein.

"Then what, oh mortal, do you offer in worship to your goddess?"

A pained expression passed across his face, and he gently held her fingertips to his lips once again. "Would that I could offer you my name, my future, my very life," he said huskily, "but I am not free. Not yet, that is, but soon, my Aphrodite, soon. It's a small matter of a marriage agreement, the result of a family arrangement which I am near to having dissolved. Once that is accomplished, however, I hope to speak of what is in my mind and heart." He squeezed her hand reassuringly.

His words suddenly brought Alicia back to reality, and she realized he still had no idea of her identity. She must needs tell him, and soon, but how, she wondered anxiously, could she explain properly at such a crowded function?

His lordship, quick to notice the small frown which had come to his lady's brow, attempted to reassure her just as the musicians struck up a country dance. "Shhh, my dear," he whispered, silencing her efforts to speak. "Let us not waste this glorious dance with serious discussion. Time enough for that later. Rather, let us relish this magic moment, for I have found my love again. This time you must not run from me, not ever again." With those words, he spun her around in dizzying response to his whirling emotions.

Lady Matilda, finally made aware of the whispers concerning her niece, turned her attention from Sir Edmund's charming company and watched in dismay as the couple danced happily together. She was at a loss to explain their change in attitude toward each other, but happy they definitely were, as anyone could see from such smiling faces. Pleased that her brother's dearest wish might yet be accomplished, she still could not condone her niece's conduct on the dance floor.

Sir Edmund, too, was surprised by his friend's actions. Certainly it was inevitable that the marquess would come to realize his mistake about the young lady, and he had refrained from trying to speed the process for fear his young friend might plant his heels in stubbornness and never acknowledge the error. But to watch his friend, apparently bewitched by the very same female as to become so oblivious to propriety that he would risk his own reputation and ruin hers, was shocking. The thought that perhaps this spectacle had been staged purposely to reap some manner of revenge, flitted across the elder gentleman's mind but was banished immediately. The expression on both their faces was too sincere, too full of devotion, for such to be the case as well as the fact that he was confident Brodhurst's character would allow no such unscrupulous behavior. No, it was evident that his friend was in love. But blast the man! Why must he choose Almack's of all places to lose his senses?

Matilda's attention was drawn from the dance floor by Lady Castlereagh placing her hand consolingly on her arm. "My dear, I have tried my best to smooth the way for Alicia's reentry into our circles, but this time my hands are tied. I fear she has done irreparable damage to herself. After her exceptionable conduct this evening, she undoubtedly will be the latest *on-dit*. Perhaps the family name and presence of a vast inheritance will serve to give her enough consequence to avoid complete ostracism, but unfortunately, my dear, I have little confidence that such will be the case."

She shook her head sadly, in sympathy with the plight of her friend. "Such want of conduct. I fear that she has sunk beneath reproach. Only an immediate betrothal could possibly redeem her, and Brodhurst will not easily be brought up to scratch."

Matilda, fanning herself in agitation, was startled by Lady Castlereagh's last statement. Quick to grasp any opportunity to save her niece from social ruin, she blurted out, unthinkingly, "But they are already betrothed. A marriage agreement was signed weeks ago." After this pronouncement her knees felt distinctly weak, and she reached out involuntarily for Sir Edmund's supporting arm.

The gentleman rose to the occasion admirably, stepping closer and smiling calmly as if nothing untoward had occurred. "A long-standing family arrangement, as I understand," he said, lending credence to Matilda's surprising announcement. "Brodhurst confided this to me some time ago. Announcement was delayed to give the couple time to become better acquainted."

"Goodness!" Lady Castlereagh exclaimed, her eyes wide in amazement upon hearing such unexpected news. "It appears that a close relationship has certainly developed." She paused, clasping her hands in excitement. "Oh, my dear, what a relief. And how very exciting for you. I simply cannot wait to tell Lady Jersey. Why, this news may actually silence Silence herself." She hurried away, stopping momentarily at each small group she passed to whisper a few quick words before moving on.

Soon the entire assembly room was buzzing again, but this time a subtle change in tone was apparent when reference was made to the Lady Alicia. Envy was still quite evident but this time tinged with respect. After all, she was soon to be the Marchioness of Brodhurst, wife of one of the most sought after bachelors in the ton.

Alicia, gloriously radiant as much from inner joy as from the exercise, was grateful when the dance came to an end. "My lord," she said breathlessly, "I am in dire need of rest and refreshment."

He gave a slight bow, offering his arm in acquiescence to her wishes. "Rest you may have, dear lady, but refreshment must wait. I refuse to leave your side before ascertaining your name." Strangely enough neither party found anything untoward in such a lack of information. "You shall not escape me again." Seeing her hesitation, he became more insistent. "Come now. Must I summon one of the hostesses to perform the introduction formally?"

Alicia, her mind racing to find a gentle way to reveal her identity and explain the situation, gathered her courage, smiled sweetly, and began. "That won't be necessary, my lord, for we have already been introduced."

"Nonsense!" he retorted. "I would have remembered." They reached the side of the room before he hesitated, looking down at her with puzzlement clearly visible in his eyes. "I will brook no more delays. Tell me now. Your name, dear lady, your name."

Alicia opened her mouth to speak, but at that moment a group of well-wishers, having just heard about the engagement, surrounded them, Lady Castlereagh being the first to speak.

"My dear boy, allow me to be the first to offer you my felicitations. I have just been informed of your betrothal to the Lady Alicia. How naughty of you to keep such news a secret, although I understand your reasons perfectly."

Brodhurst, startled that the detestable engagement

had been made public, cast a stricken glance toward his love, hoping to explain without words that this would not change his plans and that he was still determined to be free.

Baron Wycliff, an acquaintance of some years, shook the marquess's hand vigorously. "Had no idea the wind lay in that quarter, Brodhurst. Should have realized after watching the two of you dance." He winked in appreciation. "You make a fine couple."

"Why, it is simply the match of the year!" Lady Castlereagh exclaimed, taking Alicia's hand and patting it lightly. "You have my very best wishes, my dear." She then bent close to whisper, "I would suggest, however, that you exert a little more control over your feelings. Such public display of emotions on a dance floor is simply not the thing, my dear, not the thing by half."

Alicia responded to the gentle reproof by blushing deeply, an action noticed immediately by the marquess. Struggling to understand the references to both his companion and the Lady Alicia, he was stunned as he watched her countenance turn beet red. Suddenly a face from his memory, deeply scarlet with an unctuous sheen, superimposed itself over the features of his partner, and at last the realization exploded upon him. For a moment he could only stare at her in incredulity. Then an expression of pain, closely followed by anger, passed across his features before they finally attained the blank expression which was usual when he put on his accustomed air of indifference.

"Congratulations, my dear," he said quietly, his lips thin and curled in a slight sneer. "A most remarkable transformation, I must say. Any announcement of our arrangement might not have been as effective without a public display of affection. Truly a brilliant plan. Yours, or your father's? Unfortunately for you it didn't work."

Icy fingers clutched her heart as Alicia realized the meaning of his lordship's words. The light vanished from her eyes, and a cool smile that belied her inner pain froze on her lips. She dropped a slight curtsy and excused herself, only vaguely aware of the comments her actions evoked.

"Don't be angry, Brodhurst. The news was bound to leak out sooner or later. Ain't the gel's fault."

Alicia passed out of hearing, walking with dignity through the crowd, acknowledging well-wishers by an almost imperceptible nod of her head. Her regal air was as much the result of pride as it was due to an inward sense of detachment from reality. Only Matilda recognized the stricken look in her niece's eyes as the young girl approached.

"Oh, my dear, whatever is the matter?" Matilda asked, her voice full of concern.

"I can't explain," Alicia replied in a near whisper, "at least not here, not now. Oh dear. Help me, please. I feel somewhat faint."

Matilda quickly moved to support her niece and guide her to a chair by the wall, all the time wondering what could have happened to make the girl so ill.

"Forgive me for causing so much concern, but suffice it to say I must leave immediately. Where's Mr. Baugh?" She looked around quickly, conscious of a need for his unfailing devotion as well as his escort home.

"He's in the card room, I collect," Matilda responded automatically. "But, my dear, can you not be persuaded to stay a while longer? We should not leave now, not after your betrothal has been announced under such extraordinary circumstances. Such rudeness would be sheer folly and leave you open to severe criticism and gossip, a situation we have so far avoided only by the smallest of margins."

"Folly it may be, dear aunt, but I simply must get away."

"Of course, dear. If you are too ill, naturally we shall return home immediately."

Sir Edmund, who had remained Matilda's constant companion from the moment he had arrived, offered to find their young friend and hurried off toward the card room. Shortly thereafter, Geoffrey appeared at Alicia's side and informed her their carriage awaited. The young lady, too agitated to wonder at the rapidity with which their conveyance had been readied, nodded gratefully and hurried toward the door.

Matilda followed her niece, her passage somewhat slowed by questions of concern from friends at her early departure. She could only murmur excuses about suffering another headache and hurry on, hoping only for an opportunity to say goodbye to Sir Edmund. A smile of gratitude softened the lines of worry on her brow as she spied him waiting for her by the door, her cape on his arm. She knew her niece must be waiting in the carriage, but she could not resist taking one more moment to thank the gentleman for his support.

Alicia's grave expression as she donned her cape and accompanied her escort out the door had gone unnoticed by Mr. Baugh, for that gentleman's frequent need for liquid fortification had rendered him glassy-eyed and slightly dull-witted. Being in one's cups at Almack's was not to be condoned, and the young gentleman had done well to hide his condition so far. He was grateful, therefore, to accomplish so easily an early departure from the assembly room and was thoroughly convinced the Fates had decided to smile on his plans for the evening, especially when he discovered Lady Matilda had been detained for a moment, allowing him the precious moments he needed to accomplish his plan.

After speaking to the coachman for a moment, he entered the carriage and seated himself opposite the lady just before the carriage lurched and they started off at a brisk pace. Alicia noticed neither the absence of Lady Matilda nor Geoffrey's strangely disjointed movements and slightly slurred speech. She sat rigidly erect, staring out the window at the dimly lit streets with unseeing eyes.

The whole world seemed to have crumbled down around her, and just as in Humpty Dumpty no one could put it together again. She loved a man who despised her. True, he had received a false impression when he saw her recuperating from the sunburn and had certainly jumped to an insulting conclusion. But now the matter was worse, for after learning her identity, he thought her guilty of even greater trickery, all because she had not released him from that odious marriage agreement. Her little revenge had certainly turned into something less than sweet. What a muddle she had made of the entire affair.

Memories of her dance with the marquess brought a wry smile to her lips. She could once again feel the warmth of his hand on her waist and revel in the adoration visible in his eyes. Perhaps the night might have been brought to a much happier conclusion if only he had been free rather than trapped by a legal document. The smile faded as reality took hold and she acknowledged the futility of saying "if only."

Young Geoffrey watched Alicia closely as she sat, pale and mute, across from him. She had voiced no words of disapproval at his actions and must therefore be a willing participant. Boldly he took out his flask, opened it once again, and drank the last of its contents. Replacing the cap, he leaned back against the red velvet cushion, his eyes closed and a smile of satisfaction on his lips.

Alicia had no inkling that things were not as they should be until she noticed they were passing through the outskirts of the city. She looked around to question her companions and only then realized she was alone with Geoffrey.

"Where is my aunt?" she asked, her numbed mind only mildly curious about the absence of a chaperon.

"She couldn't join us," Geoffrey mumbled, still smiling. "Left her at Almack's."

His strange words roused Alicia slightly from her impassivity. "Where are we going?" she asked in a tone only slightly tinged with alarm. "This is certainly not the way to Cavendish Square. It is in the opposite direction."

His eyes opened slowly, the smile growing broader. "I know it," he stated cryptically.

"Well if you know it, why then are we heading for

Hampstead?" Her voice was low, lacking spirit. "Please turn around, Mr. Baugh, and take me home. Aunt Matilda will be worried. I am in no mood for childish pranks."

"Nothing childish about it. I'm carrying you off."

"Wh—what?" Alicia stammered, her wall of icy indifference beginning to fail. "You can't be serious."

As an answer Geoffrey nodded his head in an exaggerated manner. "Planned everything. By morning you'll have to marry me."

"Preposterous! How you could possibly have gotten such a corkbrained idea into your head, I cannot pretend to understand."

" 'Tis not a corkbrained idea," he retorted childishly.

"Mr. Baugh, you are making a cake of yourself. Take me home at once!"

"Can't," he replied, blinking repeatedly in an effort to focus her blurred outline. "Brodhurst as much as told me if I wanted you, I should carry you off. Damned fine idea. Good man, Brodhurst, a real Trojan." Giving up the struggle for clear vision, he closed his eyes once more, an inane smile fixed on his features.

"Brodhurst!" Alicia hissed. The knowledge that he was responsible for this final indignity burned through her mind. The man she loved possessed so few scruples that he would have her compromised in an effort to gain his freedom. She would not allow such a thing to happen, she promised herself.

In an effort to keep the pain of this betrayal from weakening her resolve, she steeled herself to concentrate only on a means of escape. She considered jumping from the carriage but decided against it. Although they were not traveling at a breakneck pace, the night was dark and the area unfamiliar, and she doubted she would be fortunate enough to find another carriage. Thus, leaving the protection of Mr. Baugh might bring her to a far worse fate than what she presently faced. She searched her mind frantically, hoping to come upon a suitable means of escape. With a sigh of resignation, she decided her only hope was to persuade her companion to give up this unconscionable attempt at abduction.

"Mr. Baugh, attend me. You must not do this. Brodhurst is only using you for his own unscrupulous ends. Don't you understand? Didn't you hear the prattle this evening? It is Brodhurst to whom I am betrothed."

The young gentleman failed to respond to her words, having fallen deeply asleep as a result of his overindulgence. His unconscious state became apparent when the carriage hit a rather deep rut and swayed dangerously, causing his body to slump sideways in the seat.

Relief flooded through Alicia, and she fought its accompanying weakness to garner strength enough in her voice to inform the coachman of Mr. Baugh's condition. Offering the driver double sovereigns to turn around, she settled back in her seat thankful to be heading home.

Arriving at Cavendish Square, she ran up the front steps quickly, informing a startled Babcock to pay the coachman and give directions to have the unconscious gentleman deposited at Lady Sanderson's doorstep. With a distinct air of disgust, he was about to comply with her wishes but turned back for an instant to inform her ladyship that a gentleman awaited her return in the drawing room.

Alicia opened the door hesitantly, wondering who could be visiting at such an hour. As she entered, a portly figure rose from the chair, his arms open in welcome.

The last vestige of control vanished. Tears poured from Alicia's eyes as she ran to the protection of those strong and loving arms.

"Oh, Papa," she sobbed as he cradled her gently, trying to soothe her evident pain with soft words of love and support. "Papa, things are in such a muddle. It is a coil beyond all unraveling. I have been such a goose. Oh, Papa, I love him—no, that is not true. I hate him!" Her words launched another episode of tears as she haltingly sobbed out the events of the evening, her father comforting her as best he could as the glint of anger grew brighter in his eyes.

# 9

THE MARQUESS GLANCED AGAIN at the piece of fine-grain paper in his hand before crumpling and throwing it angrily into the fireplace. "Demands to see me, does he?" his lordship muttered while pacing back and forth across his bedroom. "How dare he order me to appear!"

Then, acknowledging to himself that the Earl of Wynford did indeed have the upper hand in this situation, he called his valet and prepared to dress. He needed every moral advantage that fine attire would give him if he intended to buy off Wynford. He wished to be free of the entire matter once and for all.

His brow furrowed momentarily as the face of a goddess flitted across his mind. The vision faded, and he winced as it changed into the distasteful features of the Lady Alicia as he had seen her on the day of his visit to the Wynford estate. As yet, he was unable to ascertain the manner in which such a transformation had been accomplished, but a metamorphosis most certainly had taken place.

Although she now appeared truly lovely, her face matching the one he had carried in the secret recesses of his dreams, in his obstinacy he felt betrayed, the target of a cruel deception. He believed she had played a double trick, then made it public besides.

Somehow her disfigurement had been altered or masked. Possibly some unblemished relative—a cousin, perhaps—had been produced to trick him into going

along with the marriage. In doing so the family had be-
smirched his dream of feminine beauty, and for this
above all else he would never forgive them.

As he continued to ponder the problem, a vague feeling of things being not quite as they seemed overcame
him. Something was wrong, but try as he might, he could
not discover what it might be. That he might have made
an error in judgment, however, was unthinkable, and he
shook himself free of any nagging doubt, concentrating
on the matter at hand, which was the interview with
Alicia's father.

The marquess chose not to handle the ribbons during
the drive to Cavendish Square, preferring to sit in the
carriage contemplating the irony of the situation which
forced a marquess to bow to the demands of an earl.

His feeling of injustice, augmented by recent past
events, was not in any way lessened when Babcock
opened the door to his pull of the bell and gave the
marquess a look suitable only for a cit, and one of questionable reputation at that.

Ushered into the drawing room and announced properly, albeit with less than respectful tones, his lordship
was then given ample time to peruse his surroundings,
for the earl chose to concentrate on a document in his
hands, rather than immediately acknowledge the presence of the marquess.

Brodhurst was impressed by the decor, noticing the
newness of the satin striped upholstery and lush velvet
draperies. The furnishings were exquisite, and he wondered just how heavily in debt Granville must be after
spending so much of his blunt merely to impress visitors
such as himself.

While awaiting the earl's pleasure, Brodhurst fingered
his quizzing glass, an affectation he seldom carried except when adopting his most superior air, and examined
a Vulliany timepiece on the mantel.

The earl finally stood, cleared his throat, and strode
around the desk. Without uttering a word he handed the
document he had just been examining to Brodhurst.

The marquess glanced over the paper, realizing almost immediately that he held in his hand the very object he had been seeking these past many weeks, the dissolution of the marriage contract, written in a delicate, feminine hand and signed by the Lady Alicia. Relief flooded through him, and a broad smile of confidence replaced the bored and indifferent expression he had endeavored to maintain while being forced to wait.

"Happy to see you both have come to realize the game's at an end. You'll get much more from me this way than by trying to force me into such a ridiculous alliance," Brodhurst said as he folded the paper carefully and slipped it inside his perfectly cut coat of blue superfine. "Now, how much do you want for this release? Understand, of course, that with the paper in my possession, I am not forced to give you a single groat, but I am prepared to be magnanimous." His smile grew even wider as he leaned nonchalantly against the mantel. "Come, sir, name me a figure."

The earl had stiffened as Brodhurst began to speak. He reached out to the desk as if to steady himself. "A figure?" he asked ominously.

"Yes, a figure. How much money do you want?"

The earl's face suffused with color and his eyes closed to near slits. "How dare you offer money!" he said in a deceptively quiet voice, gripping the desk until his knuckles stood out in white relief. "Not all the blunt in the world could buy that paper!"

Brodhurst's eyes widened in surprise at the earl's reaction to his offer. The smile faded and he asked quietly, "What, then do you want from me?"

"Want? Want?" the older gentleman sputtered. "Tell you what I want. Satisfaction! That's right, young man, satisfaction!" He fairly shouted the word as he slowly approached the marquess. His rage, having been kept under control surprisingly well since the previous evening, was now given free rein. "Should have called you out long ago. Wanted to the day you insulted Alicia, but Mattie stopped me. By God! I won't be denied a second time."

The marquess was dumbfounded at the earl's surprising attack. His lips curled slightly as he wondered if the earl had lost his senses. The difference in their ages made the idea of a duel ludicrous.

Granville had stopped for a moment to catch his breath. Brodhurst, having retreated a few steps in reaction to the earl's unexpected attack, grasped the opportunity to attempt to calm the older gentleman somewhat.

"There seems to be a serious misunderstanding here, but rest assured there is no question of our engaging in a duel. I simply will not fight you." He spoke calmly in a tone meant to soothe but which was perceived as being extremely condescending by the very gentleman he had hoped to appease.

"Well, you damn well better fight," the earl snorted angrily. "Face my blade or I'll shout to the world that you, sir, are a lily-livered sapskull. Not enough bottom to face me with your corkbrained delusions, you prefer instead to believe me and my daughter capable of the lowest of deceptions. Damme, but I'm thankful your father's not here to see this."

He hesitated, eyes clouded momentarily in remembrance of his old friend, then continued, hissing his words through clenched teeth. "By God, I'd never agree to a marriage between you and my Allie now, for I want my grandchildren to have at least some semblance of intelligence. Son of my friend you may be, but I call you a half-wit, a moonling, lacking even the sense to recognize a sunburn when you see it."

Brodhurst had stiffened at this last attack, his eyes narrowing after the reference to his father, but the earl's last few words puzzled him. "A sunburn?" he questioned softly, his brow furrowed in confusion.

"Yes, a sunburn. You call to offer for my Allie, see old clothes and a red face, and immediately jump to the dunderheaded conclusion that my pockets are to let and she must needs trap a husband." The earl's rage grew as he remembered that fateful morning. "How dare you judge the gel by her face alone, when her inner beauty is radiant to all who would only look!"

Lord Granville's livid face was in sharp contrast to that of the marquess, whose features had grown pale as he listened, his eyes widening in dawning comprehension. "The Lady Alicia suffered only a temporary disfigurement? She has recovered?" he asked in a near whisper.

"From the sunburn, yes, but from your continued attacks, no. You insulted her, led her into questionable if not totally improper conduct, cut her in front of the entire assembly at Almack's, then subjected her to the indignity of an abduction."

"Abduction!" the marquess exclaimed in surprise. "I know nothing of such an occurrence."

"Refer to last night. Young man by the name of Baugh attempted to abduct my gel, at your instigation I understand. Narrow escape, that was, and damme, you'll pay for it by tasting my steel!"

Brodhurst felt a chill run through him as he began to realize the immense error in judgment which he had committed. After a slight nod, he spoke in formal tones, "My apologies, Lord Granville. You do indeed have every right to demand satisfaction. My seconds will call upon you later." With these words he turned and trod slowly from the room, his mind whirling with the surprising facts which had just been revealed to him.

Descending the front steps, he was about to enter his carriage when a phaeton approached, driven by young Baugh. Brodhurst waited until Geoffrey jumped down before speaking to him. "Answering a summons, I collect."

Geoffrey nodded glumly. "Had no idea the earl was even in town." Then, with sudden realization, he spoke quickly, "You know?"

"Unfortunately, yes," the marquess acknowledged. "The old gentleman just informed me. Hoped he was mistaken, but I see now that he had the right of it." He hesitated, noting the young man's downcast appearance. "The earl presented me with the information, yes, but then placed the responsibility squarely upon my shoulders, where it rightfully belongs, I might add."

Geoffrey looked up quickly in surprise. "Your responsibility? Oh, no. I protest. It was my mistake, and I cannot allow you to protect me."

"I am not in the habit of protecting striplings from the consequences of their actions," Brodhurst replied coolly, "nor do I go round accepting culpability for the mistakes of others. Rest easy. You have no predilection for villainy. You were merely a pawn in a much larger game. Sadly I must confess that, without giving proper consideration to the results of such efforts, I used you for my own devious plans. Mine is the main responsibility as well as the guilt. I know none of the details of your actions, nor do I wish to learn. But I sincerely apologize for having pushed you into this coil." He bowed and entered the carriage, signaling for an immediate departure to his driver.

Geoffrey watched the carriage leave, a puzzled expression on his face. Then he turned to climb the steps, flushing slightly in response to Babcock's cold and disdainful air. He entered, squaring his shoulders and lifting his chin slightly, determined to face the earl as a man, not a boy.

Lord Brodhurst sat motionless as the carriage moved briskly down Regent Street, his face pale, his eyes dark with inner pain. A small muscle quivered in his cheek as he considered the information just imparted at Wynford House.

A sunburn. Lady Alicia had suffered a sunburn, nothing more. She had never been in the position of needing to trap a husband and more important was not in financial distress, not in the least.

He had been wrong, dreadfully wrong, in his assumptions. Out of foolish pride and conceit, he had thrown away an opportunity to have his dream come true. Alicia was his ideal, his Aphrodite. Fortunate beyond most men, he had found for himself a goddess, and then foolishly denied her due homage. What could have possessed him to jump to such false assumptions? Such arrogance and false pride could no longer be overlooked.

He recalled the previous night, remembered the wondrous glow in the dear lady's eyes and how it had faded, a stricken look taking its place when upon discovering her true identity he had acted so boorishly. Her brave reaction to his cutting words and her proud bearing as she had retreated from his presence filled him with admiration. He had dealt her a death blow, and she had accepted it without a whimper.

"God! What a woman she has become," he muttered to himself, just as the carriage pulled to a stop in front of White's. Stepping down he quickly entered the select club, acknowledging greetings with a slight nod but showing no hint of a smile. His eyes searched the room slowly before he strode purposefully to a group of gentlemen standing at one side. As he approached, Sir Edmund put out his hand in welcome.

"Brodhurst, good to see you. Been wanting to have a word with you since last evening. Come, join us."

"No, thank you. I've no time. There is much for me to do, and I shall require your help. Could I persuade you to take leave of these gentlemen for a moment?"

Sir Edmund immediately made his excuses, and the two friends found a quiet corner in the morning room. As they seated themselves, Edmund noticed the haunted look in the younger man's eyes. He was about to ask the cause when Brodhurst spoke.

"I've been called out, my friend. Will you act for me?"

This revelation came as a great shock to the older gentleman, for although he acknowledged Brodhurst to be a notorious flirt, if not an out-and-out rake, the young man handled his affairs so adroitly that no duels had thus far resulted from his many escapades. Knowing that the marquess was not at the moment involved in any scandalous affair with some beautiful but bored wife of an inattentive husband, Edmund was more than taken aback by the news just presented.

"Naturally, my friend, you may count on me. But what

kind of tangle have you gotten yourself into?" Then, with surprising insight, he asked, "Does it involve the Lady Alicia?"

The marquess nodded glumly. "The earl arrived in town last night and summoned me this morning. He handed me the release I've been wanting, told me what a bufflebrain I've been, and then called me out."

Edmund stared at the young man. "Surely you're not going to fight Granville? You simply can't! The age difference—your father's friend—" His mouth worked as he tried vainly to verbalize all the reasons why such a match was out of the question.

"How well I know it," the marquess said, "and so I told him, but he forced the issue. Called me a coward if I don't face him. Then told me about the abduction and laid the responsibility for it directly at my feet."

"What abduction? Dash it! Brodhurst, what have you been up to?" Edmund asked in agitated tones, finding difficulty in keeping his voice low so as not to be overheard.

"Seems yesterday, young Baugh took my words literally and tried to abduct the Lady Alicia instead of taking her home from Almack's."

"Good Lord!" Edmund exclaimed. "It was I who detained Lady Matilda. I played right into his hand. Now it becomes clear why he was so anxious that I attend the assembly. He did, in fact, allude to the possibility that I might be needed to accompany one of the Granville ladies home."

"Well, it was I who drove her to leave the assembly early, requiring such an escort in the first place," Brodhurst countered. "Thankfully, however, there seems to have been no permanent harm done, but the earl's in a fine rage. Wants my hide, and I can't blame him. Good Lord, Edmund, I've been such a fool. Now I know what you were trying to tell me yesterday afternoon. I wouldn't listen, though. Too certain you were being bamboozled."

"I wasn't much of a friend," Edmund said, placing a hand on his friend's shoulder in comfort. "Should have pushed harder to make you see the whole of it. But, fearing you'd dig in your heels, I went easy." The older gentleman looked at the marquess solemnly before continuing. "However, we mustn't dwell on past mistakes but rather learn from them."

"Correct, my friend, and my immediate problem must be first on our minds. You must go to the earl, for I've no idea who will act for him. Then, when you discuss the arrangements, demand pistols. That should eliminate the difference in our ages."

"Good God, Brodhurst!" Edmund exclaimed. "One of you could be killed!"

"I'm aware of that," the marquess replied, his features firmly set, betraying no hint of emotion.

"But—" Sir Edmund began again in protest, only to be silenced by a quick shake of his friend's head.

"I've made my choice. It's time I accept responsibility for my actions, don't you think? See to the details, Edmund. Have no fear. Granville is safe. I go now to set my affairs in order."

It was not the earl's well-being which concerned Edmund, and his friend's last words brought a frown of worry to his forehead as they took leave of each other. After having first agreed to join Brodhurst for dinner that evening to discuss final plans, Sir Edmund reluctantly headed for Cavendish Square.

At Wynford House, Alicia stood looking out the window of the upstairs parlor, her face drawn and her eyes red and puffy. To her, last evening had been a nightmare from which she had not yet emerged. After the events of the evening, finding her father waiting with open arms had been too much for her overburdened self-control, and she had wept uncontrollably until the inner pain faded to a dull ache.

When Matilda returned, Alicia was forced to explain everything, except of course her shocking lack of conduct in the garden at the masquerade. It was impossible for her to share the glories or shame of that kiss with anyone.

Matilda had pronounced the entire situation hopeless and sent her niece off to bed, ordering a dose of laudanum for the girl to calm her nerves and allow her to sleep. Alicia still remembered kissing her papa good night and wondering at the strange hardness in his eyes, the thin, straight line of his lips, and the determined set to his jaw.

She had slept, but the morning brought no end to her pain. The actions of the marquess hurt her deeply. She despised him, or so she told herself, but still the picture of a dashing Cavalier crept into her mind, and she relived the moment when he bent low, crushing her to him, claiming her for his own. I hate him! she told herself, trying to banish the shameful memory, yet glorying in its return.

Aunt Matilda's voice broke into her thoughts. "Pray, move away from the window, dear, and come sit near me. I cannot be persuaded you do not feel a chill, for I notice a draught even over here."

Alicia drew her shawl more tightly over her shoulders, acknowledging as she did so that she did indeed feel a trifle cool, but she was strangely reluctant to leave her post at the window. She had watched the marquess leave, felt a stab of regret as his carriage disappeared into Regent Street, leaving a strange hollowness within her. Then immediately after Mr. Baugh had passed through the front door, her curiosity was piqued by the sight of a footman, envelope in hand, leaving the house and hurrying down the street.

"Something of import is occurring, Aunt Matilda, and I do so wish I knew what it was," she announced in a worried tone as she reluctantly abandoned her place at the window and took a seat on the sofa. "Lord Brodhurst has left, and Mr. Baugh is here, being raked down by Papa, I collect." She glanced over at her aunt, her eyes full of anxiety. "I can't be relieved, however. Something is afoot. I cannot shake the conviction that events are going dreadfully wrong."

"La, it's just your nerves, dear. Goodness knows you have been through a great deal, and a little depression as a result is to be expected. I must say, however, that I myself felt a trifle uncomfortable while Lord Brodhurst was here. I've no doubt that everyone in the house could at least hear your father yelling, if not understand his words completely. But he seems to have calmed himself admirably. I recall he grew quiet just before the marquess left and has remained so ever since. I'm persuaded he has matters well in hand."

Matilda placed another stitch in her embroidery, a faint frown belying her words of comfort, for she was well aware of the extent of her brother's temper, and the tangles it had led him into in the past. She had tried to calm him last night after Alicia retired, but he would have none of her company. His outburst this morning filled her with concern, but she tried to reassure her niece.

"What's happening now is something that should have occurred long ago," Matilda continued with a sigh, placing the embroidery on her lap. "Thank goodness your father's loneliness drove him to our side when it did, for after all that transpired last evening, I admit to being rather relieved to have him take charge and straighten this coil." She wrung her hands delicately. "How foolish I was to think we could teach the marquess a lesson and remain unscathed ourselves. The results of our manipulations were nearly disastrous for you, my dear. We must be thankful that your ordeal was not greater than it proved to be."

Alicia nodded glumly, unable to express an equal amount of gratitude. With a sigh, she picked up a periodical and began to peruse the latest in ladies' fashions, hoping to take her mind off the distressing topic of the Marquess of Brodhurst.

It was some time before the sound of a carriage pulling up in front of the house had both ladies looking up from their respective activities. Curiosity drove Alicia to the window once again. Standing discreetly to one side so as not to be observed, she watched a portly gentleman of rather advanced years step down from the carriage and make to enter the house.

"Why, it's Lord Worthington," she exclaimed. "It's been an age since I've seen him—not since gout put an end to his riding to the hounds with Papa."

"I wonder what brings him here?" Matilda asked, her brow knitted in puzzlement, "unless he has heard already your father is in town, and I've certainly no idea how such information reached him. If we are to receive guests, however, perhaps you should try to make yourself more presentable, dear."

Alicia agreed and returned to her room, summoning her maid with a pull of the bell rope. Mary answered immediately, her hands fluttering in agitation.

"Oh, m'lady, it's a terrible thing that's happening. All downstairs is talking about it. What your papa could be a'thinkin', I'll never know, his age being what it is and all. . . ."

"Whatever are you talking about, Mary. What has my father done?" Alicia asked, alarmed, all thoughts of clothing vanishing from her mind.

"I thought for certain you knew, m'lady, what with your papa yelling so loud and all. I'm sure it's not my place to be telling you," she said, pursing her lips as if determined to say no more.

"Mary!" Alicia snapped, stamping her foot in exasperation. "Tell me this moment. What has happened?"

"If you insist," the maid answered reluctantly, "but Mr. Babcock will ring a peal over me if he finds out, not to mention the earl, for I'm sure he'd not be wanting me to tell."

"Yes, yes. Don't worry. No one will find out, I promise. But if you don't speak up immediately, I will be the one to ring a peal, and that's another promise."

Mary nodded, swallowed nervously, and looked sadly at her mistress as she spoke in a near-whisper. "There's to be a duel, m'lady. Your papa's called out the marquess."

"A duel? You must be mistaken," Alicia replied firmly. "Papa would never do such a thing." She spoke these last words with a note of finality. Then, remembering her father's temper and the strange look in his eyes last night, she felt the need to amend her statement. "Even if he did, the marquess would never allow such a thing to occur. He would refuse, I'm sure of it."

"Well, your papa did, and Lord Brodhurst accepted. We all heard it." Mary began to wring her hands in worry.

"Goodness, this cannot be. It simply mustn't. I won't let such a thing happen." Alicia's words sounded firm and controlled, but her heart was pounding from shock and fear.

"Oh m'lady, whatever can you do?" Mary asked, near to tears.

"I'm sure I don't know, but there must be something. Aunt Matilda may be able to help." The words had barely left Alicia's lips before she was hurrying out the door and down the stairs to the small parlor.

Matilda noticed her niece's agitation immediately and demanded to know its cause. Upon hearing the startling news, she dismissed the entire story as a Banbury tale. After Alicia summoned Mary to recount the details again, however, the lady rose and stated flatly that she would speak to her brother immediately in hopes of bringing him to his senses before it was too late.

Alicia accompanied her aunt, after having reassured a terrified Mary that they would not disclose their source of information, an easy task since her father had shouted loudly enough for any number of people to hear.

Learning from a footman that the earl was closeted in the library with Lord Worthington, the two ladies proceeded to the drawing room to await his lordship's pleasure. They were in deep discussion, hoping to come upon the best argument to dissuade the earl from his disastrous course, when Babcock announced Sir Edmund Coswell.

"Why, Sir Edmund, how nice to see you," Matilda said, flashing a brilliant smile of welcome. "You always seem to appear when I most need a friend."

"At your service, ladies," he said, smiling broadly and making a gallant bow. "You have but to ask. What seems to be the problem?" It was his intent to keep secret from the ladies the serious reason for his visit to Wynford House, and so he acted the part of a complete innocent. "I certainly hope you have recovered from your indisposition of last night," he said to Alicia, choosing his words with the intent of creating an opening for the ladies to impart any information they might deem proper for him to receive.

"To a certain extent, yes, thank you," Alicia replied enigmatically as she exchanged speaking glances with her aunt.

Matilda, unable to contain her agitation, continued to explain. "She has undergone a great deal in the past few days, and I fear there is much more to endure. For a new situation has developed which has us both in a quandary." The lady hesitated, plainly unsure if she should continue.

"Perhaps I should not divulge our problem, but we need assistance in straightening out a terrible coil. Since you are a close friend of Lord Brodhurst, perhaps you are the very one who can aid us in accomplishing our purpose. You see, there is to be a duel, and—"

"Details of that matter, unfortunately, have already been divulged to me," Sir Edmund broke in, the gravity of his manner showing that he did indeed have full acquaintance with the situation.

"You know?" both ladies queried in unison, their startled faces displaying mixed emotions. After a moment's hesitation, Alicia was the first to come to the appropriate conclusion.

"Lord Brodhurst told you, then," she stated rather than asked. "You are here on his behalf."

Edmund nodded in answer, allowing this information to be thoroughly understood before explaining further.

"But you simply can't be," Matilda responded. "Surely Lord Brodhurst doesn't intend to continue with this insane idea?"

"Unfortunately he is quite determined to see it through," Edmund replied, becoming distinctly uncomfortable with the turn of the conversation.

"But you must stop it!" Alicia exclaimed. "Papa's temper is atrocious and sometimes does him a great disservice, I know, but eventually he always comes round. Surely the marquess would understand that."

"A second's duty is to attempt a reconciliation, of course, and I shall certainly make every effort in that regard. Unfortunately, after having just spoken to Lord Brodhurst, it is my opinion that he will not be persuaded to turn away from this course."

"Fustian!" Matilda snapped in exasperation. "Is it left, then, to the women to make them see their folly?"

Sir Edmund, convinced that enough had been said on the subject, valiantly sought to terminate the conversation or, at the very least, to change its direction. "I respectfully submit that both of you withdraw and let the gentlemen handle their affairs in their own way. I scarcely think the earl will be pleased to hear that you are even aware of what is to transpire. How *did* you learn of it, by the way?"

Matilda waved her hand as if to brush aside the question. "It doesn't signify. Of import is the fact that my brother may put an end to his own life, if not that of another. Foolish pride," she adjudged, tapping her foot in exasperation.

Although inwardly agreeing with her, Edmund was forced to defend the actions of gentlemen. "Feminine minds seldom comprehend the finer points of honor," he pronounced solemnly.

Matilda stiffened at this remark and was about to loose a sharp rejoinder, when a deep voice sounded from the doorway.

"Well said, sir. My compliments." The Earl of Wynford strode briskly into the room. "Ladies, there is no business here for you. We shall speak later." He waved them away and turned to greet Sir Edmund formally, introducing Lord Worthington, who had followed him into the room, as his second.

The two ladies exited with heads held high and eyes snapping in anger and frustration. Upon reaching the confines of the small parlor, Matilda stamped her foot in frustration. "To be banished in such a fashion is humiliating in the extreme."

Alicia agreed with her aunt, and they broke into animated conversation, upbraiding the men in their lives for such foolish actions, as well as themselves for having instigated the situation which finally resulted in this predicament. Unfortunately, search as they might, they were unable to come upon a solution to the problem.

"There is one thing I simply must do," Matilda said, shattering the silence which had finally settled upon the ladies as they contemplated the sad affair to come. "I shall immediately cancel our planned excursion to the botanical gardens. We surely cannot let ourselves be accompanied by a gentleman who has recently tried to abduct you and another who feels we have no business trying to eliminate bloodshed."

She took a small handkerchief from her sleeve and dabbed at her eyes. "I own to being very disappointed with Sir Edmund," she confessed with a delicate sniff, "and I shall be very angry with your father, as soon as I'm assured of his safety, that is."

Alicia tried to comfort her aunt, but was unable to banish her own worry, for she feared for the safety of not only her father but the odious Lord Brodhurst as well.

Early the following morning a carriage lumbered along the road leading to the hamlet of Westbourn Green. Sir Edmund sat ignoring his companions, gazing out the window at the gently rolling countryside, his arm resting on a slim case containing a set of dueling pistols. He contemplated the letters which rested in his pocket, one addressed to a solicitor and the other to the Dowager Marchioness, which Lord Brodhurst had given him to deliver in the event of his death. An unexpected chill overtook him, and he shivered, knowing full well that such a possibility was always present when two men faced each other with pistols drawn.

Moving as if to shake off such morbid thoughts, he felt

the presence of a small package in the other pocket, another item he was to deliver. But this one was meant for the Lady Alicia and was to be bestowed into her hands after the duel.

Finally the carriage pulled to a stop on the road. Sir Edmund jumped down, followed by a tall, thin gentleman carrying a black case of such singular size and shape as to label its owner a distinguished member of the medical profession.

A third gentleman stepped down gracefully, his fluid movements giving the impression of careless disregard for the seriousness of the moment. Lord Brodhurst's face, however, spoke a great deal of his inner thoughts, giving the impression of a certain maturity having been attained overnight. His eyes were hooded, but the lines at either side of his mouth accented a determined set to his jaw.

The trio started across the field to join the figures awaiting them on a gentle rise, silhouetted by the gray light of an overcast dawn. The air was cool, and a light mist rose from the damp earth. Chilled as much by the scene as the temperature, Sir Edmund tried to shake off the sense of foreboding which had filled him from the first moment he had awakened that morning.

"Don't like it by half, my friend. Is there no other way?"

Brodhurst shook his head sadly, but said nothing.

"I'm persuaded Granville's no crack shot, so you should have the best of it. Try not to kill him, though. I'd hate to make arrangements for your quick flight to the Continent, let alone face the ladies after such an occurrence.

The marquess glanced quickly at his friend, reading a deeper meaning behind the words just spoken. "I shall not kill him, of that you can be certain."

Instead of reassuring him, the statement served only to accentuate Sir Edmund's uneasiness, but he was prevented from speaking further by a motion for silence from the marquess as they reached their destination.

The Earl of Wynford, stamping about in impatience to get on with the affair as well as in an effort to keep warm, moved forward quickly to greet them. A formal salute between the two principals was accomplished, and Lord Worthington, the earl's second, helped to load the set of perfectly balanced dueling pistols which Sir Edmund had furnished. Hardly a word was spoken while the seconds measured off the paces, twenty in number, and then delivered the weapons to the combatants before moving away to leave the area clear for the duel.

Both principals were dressed in black, their coats buttoned up to the throat. They stood presenting their sides to each other, their arms down, pistols at half-cock.

Small beads of perspiration appeared on the earl's forehead as he glared at his opponent, his left hand twitching slightly in agitation. Lord Brodhurst, in contrast, appeared unmoved as he stared calmly at the earl, his face pale against his dark clothing.

For a moment, all grew quiet. Even the birds stopped their incessant chirping. Sir Edmund held up a white handkerchief which fluttered slightly in the gentle breeze, and after judging the gentlemen ready and the time appropriate, let it drop.

Both men raised their pistols, but Brodhurst moved more quickly, pointing his weapon straight up and firing into the air.

"Good God! The man has deloped!" Lord Worthington exclaimed in a muffled voice, his mouth remaining open in astonishment.

"A tacit acknowledgment of being in the wrong," Sir Edmund responded, his mouth dry from anxiety for his friend. "Will your man accept it?"

Lord Worthington shook his head. "Doubt it. The man's a terror when his temper pushes him. Feels things have gone too far, I own. But must confess the possibility of an apology was never discussed."

Lord Granville, startled at first by Brodhurst's unexpected action into dropping his aim, brought his arm up again slowly and took careful aim upon the figure opposite him, his anger at the man who had brought his daughter to such a display of tears still unappeased. He held his arm stiff, his jaw tightly clenched, and his lips pressed into a fine line. An eternity seemed to pass as he stared down the sights at the marquess.

"Blast it all! I can't shoot an unarmed man!" he shouted and threw his weapon on the ground in exasperation. The half-cocked pistol fired upon impact, and Lord Brodhurst crumpled to the ground.

# $==10==$

THE FRONT DOOR OF Wynford House burst open, startling Alicia and her aunt who were descending the stairs, intent upon a morning walk to help calm their minds and banish some of the fear which had been present since the first mention of a duel.

Lord Granville rushed in, barking orders as he handed hat and gloves to Babcock. "You there," he pointed at a hapless footman, "go help the gentlemen outside." He turned to Babcock. "Have Cook send up warm water and clean cloths. We have a wounded man to attend." He looked up, spying the two ladies and waved them off with his hand.

"Out of the way," he ordered, then changed his mind. "Better yet, see to it a bedroom is ready for our guest. Quickly now."

Without a word, Matilda turned and hurried back up the stairs. Alicia was about to do the same when the door opened once more. Her face drained of color as she saw Lord Brodhurst being supported by Sir Edmund and the footman and followed closely by a gentleman carrying a black case, whom she presumed to be the doctor.

The marquess walked slowly, his arms draped over the shoulders of his helpers. His head, covered by a makeshift bandage which was soaked through with blood, hung down as if too heavy to be supported. As they reached the staircase, he looked up, aware that Alicia was staring at him.

"Your servant," he mumbled, attempting a wan smile as the trio passed her on their way up to the stairs.

Alicia followed the gentlemen to a bedroom at the end of the corridor, her bosom heaving with conflicting emotions. She was relieved that her father was unhurt and that no one was killed, but the depth of her pain upon seeing the injured marquess was totally unexpected.

Matilda stood holding open the door to a large bedroom. "Put him in here," she said. "The room has recently been aired, and I've had a maid turn down the bed."

As the group made to enter, she caught her brother's arm and pulled him to one side, bombarding him with questions as she did so. Alicia joined them, lending her voice to the shower of questions raining down upon the earl.

Having expected such a reaction, Lord Granville was not flustered, only impatient, and answered with extreme brevity.

"Shot him by accident. Not as bad as it appears. Couldn't leave him at his own place. Valet no help at all. One look at Brodhurst and the damned fool fainted dead away. Couldn't stomach the sight of blood, I own. Responsible for the man's condition, so had no other choice. Brought him here to get proper care. Least I can do."

This disjointed explanation was too much for Alicia. She placed both hands against her temples, shaking her head slowly, unable to comprehend exactly what had happened.

"An accident," she repeated in disbelief. "How could it have been an accident when you both went out this morning with the express purpose of shooting each other? Now he lies in there, wounded. What's more, he could have been killed, yet you call it an accident? Ridiculous!"

Matilda and her brother exchanged speaking glances. The reasons behind the girl's extreme reaction were suspect. A glimmer of understanding brought a smile to the earl's lips.

"An accident it was, Allie, and traced directly to my

confounded temper. Brodhurst had no intention of fighting, but meant only to give me satisfaction. Why, the
man deloped. Took courage. More than I gave him credit
for, I'll be bound. Restored my faith in him. Good man,
Brodhurst. A little confused in his thinking, but straightened around now, I'd say. No doubt he's sorry for all
that's happened." The earl cast a worried glance at the
closed door before continuing. "I confess I am."

Just then a maid carrying a basin of water and spong-
ing cloths passed them and stopped at the bedroom. The
door opened to her knock and she quickly disappeared,
emerging again within moments, followed by the footman and Sir Edmund.

The latter stopped to join the group standing watch in
the corridor and made a preliminary report. "We have
him resting comfortably, now. Seems to be only a minor
wound. He'll be up and about in a day or two at the most,
mark my words."

"Let us pray you are correct," Matilda replied, "but I
cannot be relieved until the doctor pronounces him out
of danger."

"We can't just stand out here waiting until he does so,"
the earl stated flatly. "I, for one, could stand some breakfast."

The group repaired downstairs to the drawing room
until breakfast could be made ready. Shortly thereafter,
the physician joined them and pronounced the marquess
in good condition under the circumstances.

"Lucky man, Lord Brodhurst," he commented. "Bullet
just creased his temple. He'll have a headache, to be sure.
Might have suffered a concussion. Keep him quiet. Fever
will come up, too, so keep a good watch. If all goes well,
he should recover nicely."

"Thank goodness." Lady Matilda voiced the opinions
of the entire group. The physician took his leave and she
led the procession into the dining room. "I own to having
felt a trifle faint from fear and worry since the first moment I arose this morning. Seeing you safe, dear brother,
was gratifying. The thought, however, that you may

have killed a man, an unarmed one at that, was quite distressing."

"Humph," Lord Granville grunted, helping himself to some kidneys from the sideboard. "Distressing to me as well."

"I should hope so," Matilda replied tartly. "Explain to me, please, why someone should delope, as you say, when he is taking part in a ritual expressly designed to do physical harm to the principals in it."

Sir Edmund chose to answer, still acting as second for the gentleman in question. "Deloping is a formal acknowledgment of being in the wrong," he explained.

"Oh? Much the same as an apology?" Alicia asked, joining her aunt in questioning the entire affair.

"Why, yes, in a manner of speaking," Sir Edmund replied.

Both Alicia and her aunt were confused. "Then why did not Lord Brodhurst apologize yesterday, thus avoiding the entire situation?" Alicia continued.

"But, dear lady," Edmund countered, "to stand in front of one's adversary unarmed and admitting guilt is quite courageous."

"Yes, yes," the earl added. "Most honorable."

Matilda looked first at her brother and then to Sir Edmund. "I confess to being totally confused at this entire affair," she stated. "To me, standing in front of an armed opponent, waiting to be shot, is the height of folly."

Sir Edmund was at a loss for words with which to respond to so logical a statement. Lord Granville came to his rescue. " 'Twas my actions which were the height of folly, Matilda. Even a moonling should know better than to handle a cocked pistol in such a manner."

"Oh, then, am I to assume that you should have shot the marquess on purpose instead of accidentally?" Matilda queried in an innocent tone.

The earl hesitated before answering, not certain of where his sister was leading. "Yes, I suppose you could say that. At least it's not quite the thing."

"If it would have been dishonorable for you to shoot

him, then why was it courageous of him to stand before you unarmed?"

"Madame, you are being purposely obtuse," the earl said in exasperation. "Making a simple matter into something extremely complicated."

"No, dear brother. I am only confirming Sir Edmund's opinion that female minds seldom comprehend the finer points of honor. Those were your very words, were they not, Sir Edmund?" she asked, turning to the gentleman with an expression of exaggerated innocence.

He nodded and she continued. "Yes, you were certainly correct. I do not understand. No one can convince me that dueling is anything but folly. The law is in agreement, I do believe, for has not the practice been declared illegal?"

Her telling blow delivered, Matilda sat back, a smile of satisfaction on her lips. The earl coughed nervously, muttering his acknowledgment out of embarrassment.

Sir Edmund smiled in admiration. "*Touché,*" he said quietly, bringing an even broader smile accompanied by a dimple to Matilda's cheek. She nodded acceptance of his compliment and set to buttering a warm muffin, happy to have defended feminine honor successfully.

Unfortunately, Alicia took no notice of her aunt's victory, having lost interest in the repartee as she considered the marquess and his actions. She sat deep in thought, munching absently on a piece of toast. The presence of Lord Brodhurst in Wynford House, injured and relatively helpless, was disturbing. She had run the gamut of emotions: shock and fear upon his arrival in such a condition, anger at the entire situation, and relief upon hearing the doctor's prognosis. She was making a valiant effort to maintain her degree of anger at the odious marquess but surprisingly found the task difficult in the extreme.

Her problem was greatly increased that evening when she looked in on the patient to find Mary struggling to hold a thrashing Lord Brodhurst on the bed.

"Oh, m'lady, it's the fever. He's delirious," the maid explained.

Alicia quickly joined the girl by the bedside, speaking softly to the marquess as she wet a cloth and placed it on his burning forehead. The touch of the cool towel accompanied by her soothing voice seemed to calm the injured man, and soon he was resting quietly.

"Go get your dinner," Alicia ordered her maid. "I shall stay until I'm assured he will remain quiet. Perhaps arrangements can be made to have Papa's valet watch him through the night. Jenkins can be trusted not to faint away. He has proven himself often, nursing Papa through several riding accidents."

The maid left gladly, but sent a footman to stand guard and help her mistress should the marquess become violent again. Before seeing to her meal, however, she searched out Jenkins and explained the problem. The valet sniffed haughtily, announcing that the earl had already requested his aid in the matter and that a pallet would be laid in the room shortly, thus allowing him to rest until needed to tend the invalid. Mary smiled, happy to have served her mistress successfully, and proceeded to the kitchen, intent upon her evening meal which had been greatly delayed.

Alicia sat quietly, watching the sleeping figure, her thoughts filled with a myriad "if only's." If only she had not been sunburned on that most inauspicious day. If only her father had not allowed the marquess to see her in such a condition. If only he had not jumped to such silly conclusions. If only she had not sought revenge. On and on, over and over, her thoughts flew through the events of the past few weeks, returning always to one final "if." If only she did not love him so. She hung her head in acknowledgment of the truth. She loved the marquess with all her heart and soul. He had hurt her, wounded her deeply time and time again. She could not condone his actions, but still she loved him deeply. No matter what happened, he would be a part of her thoughts, her very life from this moment on.

As if reading her mind, Lord Brodhurst became restless, muttering in his sleep. Alicia bent low to hear his words.

"Alicia . . . Aphrodite . . . love the woman . . . foolish mortal . . . unworthy . . . love Alicia . . . " He trailed off, relaxing once more into a quiet sleep.

Alicia's heart was singing. That she had heard the words clearly could not be doubted, and although spoken out of feverish delirium, she was certain they sprang from truth. He loved her. Those golden words eased the pain of all that had gone on before. She had acknowledged her love for him and now discovered he returned the emotion. Somehow everything would work itself out to a satisfactory conclusion, she was certain of it.

Hugging this glorious knowledge within her, she continued her watch of his bedside until, Jenkins having relieved her, she slipped out of the room and retired for the night. She drifted asleep quickly, her face wreathed in smiles as she recalled his words over and over: "Love Alicia, love Alicia. . . ."

She was still smiling when Mary looked in on her mistress the next morning, and the smile stayed on her features during the entire day. Both the earl and his sister were at a loss to explain her extremely sunny attitude, her enthusiastic support of any activity which was suggested, and her constant humming as she went about the house.

Lord Brodhurst's valet arrived during the day to take charge of the invalid. Since the wound was healing nicely and the presence of bloody bandages was no longer a problem, the gentleman's gentleman could now be trusted to attend his master.

The fever broke early the following morning, and it was clear his lordship was on the mend. By evening he was in fine fettle, refusing the broth deemed appropriate for convalescents and demanding that food more suitable for masculine appetites be brought before him immediately.

Alicia had no opportunity to see him alone and, accompanied by her aunt, was only allowed to visit him briefly, at which time she was quick to express her pleasure at finding him so much improved.

The marquess, somewhat embarrassed at being an unexpected guest in their house, extended his apologies for any inconvenience he might have caused. Both ladies quickly denied any problems due to his visit, and upon hearing his stated desire to immediately remove himself to his own quarters and fearing that a move so soon might aggravate his condition, quickly worked to convince him that he should stay. Both his valet and Sir Edmund, as well as the earl, supported them in this with the happy result that the marquess remained at Wynford House one more day.

The following morning Alicia and her aunt waited in the small parlor for Lord Brodhurst to appear and take his leave of them, the surgeon having already departed after arriving early and pronouncing his patient well enough to quit his bed.

Sir Edmund was announced, and upon being apprised of his friend's recovery, expressed his pleasure at being present to offer any aid in making the move a smooth and uncomplicated matter.

"Oh, I'm certain his valet has matters well in hand," Lady Matilda commented, "but I collect the marquess would welcome your company on the journey back to his lodgings."

"As I would his," Sir Edmund replied. "I must, however, complete the business which brought me here." He appeared uncomfortable and ill at ease, much altered from his usual easy manner, and he brought forth a small package, handing it to Alicia.

"Brodhurst gave this into my safekeeping before the duel, asking that I give it to you in the event anything should happen to him. As we all know, unfortunately such was the case. But due to all the excitement and worry, the matter slipped my mind until today. Please forgive the delay."

"Of course, Sir Edmund, you need not have asked. Please do not let yourself be bothered another moment," Alicia assured him, accepting the package calmly with a gracious "Thank you," and attempting with difficulty to control her curiosity.

"Perhaps you would care to examine it in privacy," the gentleman suggested, noticing the gleam of excitement in her eyes. "Besides, I have something of import to discuss with your aunt."

"Oh. Of course. I shall leave you alone then," Alicia said, wondering at Matilda's bright smile and quick attempts to smooth her skirts and hide an unruly curl.

As she closed the door, she noticed Sir Edmund bending low over Matilda's hand and questioned why he should be acting in such a courtly manner. Anxious to see what was in the package, however, she put aside the intriguing puzzle and was about to ascend to the third floor and her own room when she noticed Babcock ascending from below.

"M'lady," he said, spying her in the corridor. "Mr. Baugh is downstairs and requests an audience with you. He says it will only take a few moments of your time if you will be so gracious as to receive him."

"Of course I will see him," Alicia replied, curious as to why the young man should return so soon after his interview with her father. "Is he in the drawing room?"

Babcock answered in the affirmative, and she proceeded down the stairs, secreting the small package in her pocket with the thought of examining it at a later time.

Geoffrey was standing by the fireplace when she entered. When he turned to greet her, she was shocked at the suffering she read in his eyes. He did not wait for her to speak but walked swiftly to her side, dropped to one knee, and caught her hand up to his lips.

"My lady," he said with reverence. "I come to humbly beg your forgiveness. My actions were despicable, and I have no excuse. But I wish you to know that I heartily repent of them and promise never to allow drink to fog my brain again."

She colored prettily at his speech, then made to brush away the entire affair with a flick of her hand. "Oh, Mr. Baugh, please do get up. Of course I shall forgive you. The entire matter is nearly forgotten. I own you have suffered enough already, having survived a severe lecture by my father." She smiled sympathetically, then seated herself and folded her hands primly in her lap after motioning for Geoffrey to follow her lead and accept a seat in the adjacent chair. "Was it too bad?" she asked gently.

"It was rather uncomfortable, I confess, but the earl did seem to understand and suggested I refrain from indulging in strong drink for quite some time. I collect perhaps he was swayed somewhat by the fact that I did mean marriage and was eloping, not to escape his disfavor, but rather as the only way to win your hand. He amazed me by saying that he would approve of the marriage if you wanted it." He stopped, swallowed, and squared his shoulders.

"That is why I have come. I could not rest until I have pressed you for an answer. Lady Alicia, will you do me the great honor of becoming my wife?" Having spoken those words, he heaved a great sigh of relief, then watched his beloved closely, waiting anxiously for an answer.

Alicia, taken completely by surprise, was unable to think clearly for a moment. Then, carefully fashioning her reply, spoke soothingly, desiring not to hurt this suitor more than was necessary.

"Thank you, Mr. Baugh. You do me a great honor by asking. I must, however, refuse. I am persuaded we would not suit, for although I hold you as a friend, I do not love you. Please, let us forget this ever happened and go on as before."

Geoffrey shook his head, accepting her rejection in a resigned manner. "No. I feared you would never accept my offer, but to bring peace of mind I deemed it necessary to ask formally before starting my journey north."

"You are quitting London?" Alicia asked with concern.

"Shouldn't you stay and finish out the Season. Some lovely lady might still catch your eye."

"No, I think not. Having little hope of receiving an affirmative reply to my suit, I used my inheritance to buy a commission. I head north in the morning to take leave of my father before journeying across the Atlantic and joining the fight against those upstart colonials."

"America!" Alicia exclaimed. "Must you go so far?"

The young man nodded solemnly. "Looking forward to it as a matter of fact. An exciting country, or so I've been told. Father fought there in his youth before inheriting the title, and I rather think he will be proud of me."

"If your mind is made up, then I wish you every success." She proffered her hand once more, and Geoffrey caught it to his lips.

"Goodbye, dear lady," he said huskily and left the room.

Alicia sat for a moment in silence, pondering what had just occurred. She was sad to see him go, yet relieved that neither would be a source of embarrassment to the other again, for embarrassed they both were. Their easy relationship had been lost, and she doubted it would ever be regained.

She also considered her reaction to the young man's formal offer of marriage. Never would she have believed herself capable of so much poise as to reject a proposal in such a manner as to spare her suitor's feelings. She had certainly matured, an event not at all surprising considering all that had transpired in the past few days. Confidence comes with facing and overcoming difficult situations, and this she had most certainly accomplished. Her thoughts naturally turned to the difficulties experienced in her relationship with Lord Brodhurst, and she suddenly remembered the package still lying unopened in her pocket.

Retrieving it quickly, she sat down and examined the present. It was small and wrapped in plain paper which she quickly tore away, revealing a lovely blue velvet box. Upon opening it, she discovered a small note. "Forgive me," it said simply and was unsigned. Under the note was nestled a small golden apple on a delicate golden chain.

"How lovely," she whispered to herself, examining it closely, admiring the craftsmanship exhibited and wondering at the work involved in fashioning such an exquisite piece of jewelry. For a moment she did not realize its significance, but soon recalled the night of the masquerade when her Cavalier had called her Aphrodite. In the myth, Paris had given Aphrodite a golden apple. Thus the marquess was calling her his goddess, just as he had done that night while his fever raged. This was his manner of paying homage as well as saying good-bye.

He had not expected to survive, she knew, or he would not have given her such a present. Unfortunately propriety dictated, as he was certainly aware, that she not accept it. Of course, she reminded herself, it had reached her hands under unusual circumstances. Perhaps an argument could be made in favor of retaining the present.

She quickly ran upstairs, anxious to show Aunt Matilda her tiny gift and determine if there was a possibility of her keeping it. Rushing into the small parlor, she was just in time to interrupt an intimate embrace between her aunt and Sir Edmund.

"Oh! Ah, excuse me," Alicia said, coloring in embarrassment. "I own it was too bad of me to enter without knocking. I shall come back later." She made to back out the door, but Matilda stopped her.

"Pray, don't leave us, dear," she called out. "We have something of import to announce." She glanced up at Sir Edmund with adoring eyes.

"Yes," the gentleman continued, clearing his throat in a nervous manner and staring at the floor, hesitant to speak. "You see, ah, your aunt has just consented to be my wife. Ah, I shall soon be your uncle. You have no objections, I hope."

Alicia was taken aback. She had known the two of them were getting along rather well, but having been so involved with her own situation, she had given little thought to anyone else. Now, after having just declined an offer of marriage herself, she was presented with the startling information that her aunt had accepted one. Forgetting all about the golden apple which she clasped tightly in her hand, she ran to Matilda, embracing her joyfully.

"I can be nothing but happy for you," she said simply. "How wonderful that you have found each other." She turned to Sir Edmund. "Of course I have no objections. You will make a wonderful uncle. I confess I rather think of you as one already. Welcome to the family," she said and stood on tiptoe to kiss him on the cheek.

"I seem to be interrupting an intimate moment," a deep voice broke in on the happy scene.

Alicia turned quickly, coloring deeply when she saw the tall figure of the marquess standing in the doorway.

"Come in, my dear fellow," Sir Edmund said. "Congratulate me, for the dear lady has accepted my offer. I am to be married."

His lordship appeared surprised for a moment. A small muscle quivered in his cheek, and his eyes grew cold as he made a slight bow to his friend. "My sincere felicitations, Edmund. I wish you both every happiness."

"Come, come, you can do better than that. I know your injury does not preclude a smile. Is it perhaps that you feel I am making a mistake?"

Lord Brodhurst's lips curved slightly. "Certainly not. I could not suggest a better choice than the lady who has accepted you. My reaction was not due to any misgivings but rather a result of my envy for your good fortune."

Edmund smiled broadly. "Much better," he said, accepting the offered hand of the marquess in a firm clasp of friendship. Then he turned to Matilda. "Perhaps we should leave these two alone for a moment. I'm persuaded they have much to say to each other." Then, in a voice meant for her ears only, he whispered, "Fetch your pelisse. I shall await you downstairs."

Matilda agreed happily and said her goodbyes to the marquess before quitting the room. Sir Edmund followed immediately behind. Alicia stood alone before Lord

Brodhurst, ill at ease yet reveling in this moment of near-ness to the man she loved.

"Won't you sit down?" she asked, moving to the sofa near her.

"No, I cannot stay. I only came to make my farewells and to ask your forgiveness."

Alicia was disappointed that he meant to go so quickly but, with hope remaining strong, worked to detain him a while longer. "My lord, you have already been forgiven. I received your note and the lovely necklace. It is so beautiful. You have my gratitude for such a thoughtful gift, but unfortunately I fear I may not accept it." She opened her hand and held out the golden apple, sadness and disappointment written on her face as she offered to return it.

"A mere bauble," he announced, "intended only to amuse. A trinket with no great meaning, I assure you. There is no reason not to keep it." He spoke sternly as if reproving a child.

"Oh," she said, experiencing a familiar sinking sensa-tion once again. "I had no idea. Yes, it is amusing. Thank you again."

"You are most welcome," he replied, then made to move toward the door. "I must take my leave. Thank you for your generous hospitality. You shan't be bothered by my presence further. I doubt we shall meet again."

"Why, whatever do you mean? Surely we shall see each other from time to time, at least during the remain-der of the Season?"

"No, that will not be the case," the marquess replied, shaking his head slowly. "It is my decision to join my mother on the Continent. Perhaps the grand tour will do me good."

"But are you recovered enough for such a strenuous journey?" she asked anxiously, hoping somehow to dis-suade him from such an undertaking. If he left England, how could they possibly reconcile their differences? "Surely you will not travel until you have recuperated fully."

"A matter of only a few days at the most," Brodhurst replied. "Then I shall no longer be around to bring you pain. I am sincerely repentant for all my actions, dear lady, and I hope that you will be very happy. My felicitations." With these words he turned on his heel and walked quickly out the door.

Alicia, tempted to run after him, stood quietly, her pride keeping her from such precipitous action. She looked at the tiny apple in the palm of her hand. A bauble, he had called it. A trinket of no great import, intended only to amuse. She had misread its meaning entirely and smarted from the knowledge. Tears welled up from within and quietly began to spill over.

Lord Brodhurst found the earl, Sir Edmund, and Lady Matilda talking in front of the house. A footman opened the carriage door, and Matilda made to enter. Sir Edmund clasped the earl's hand, then turned to join her.

"And where are you off to, my friend?" Brodhurst asked before Edmund could enter the carriage. "Surely you're not leaving the Lady Alicia alone?"

"Most certainly. I plan to escort Matilda on a tour of the botanical gardens, an unfulfilled dream of hers. It will be our first excursion as an engaged couple."

The earl added his comments. "Yes, and don't they make a fine pair? I gave them my blessing, as if they needed it, but it pleases me to see Mattie so happy."

Lord Brodhurst was startled. "Let me get this straightened in my mind. Am I to understand that you are engaged to the Lady Matilda?" he asked his friend. "You have never been interested in Alicia?"

Sir Edmund nodded in answer to the first question, then shook his head in shocked disbelief while replying to the second. " 'Pon my word. How could you have entertained such a thought? Alicia, to be sure, is a lovely young lady, and I shall be proud to have her as a niece, but that has been my only interest, with the exception, however, that I always believed you two to be admirably suited for each other."

"Yes, my opinion exactly," Lord Granville added. "In

fact, I happen to believe that she has definitely developed a *tendre* for you, young man. How could you have thought she would wed Sir Edmund?"

"I have been an idiot once more," Brodhurst announced, "but never again!" He turned and entered the house, taking the stairs in three bounds, ignoring the pounding headache which returned as a result of such strenuous exercise while he was still unwell.

He entered the small parlor to find Alicia still there, a small, dejected figure sitting on the sofa facing away from the door, her head down, her hands clasped to her bosom.

"Alicia," he whispered huskily.

Her head jerked up at the sound of his voice, her eyes wide with the realization that he had used her given name. She stood and moved away from the sofa but did not turn to face him.

"Alicia, I have been such a fool, an idiot who never learns from past mistakes. How can I have treated you so badly? Only minutes ago, believing you and Edmund were betrothed, I almost left your side forever without declaring myself. My error, thankfully, was pointed out to me, and I have returned to rectify the situation." He walked slowly toward her, coming to a stop directly behind the young lady.

"I love you with all my heart," he whispered huskily, his voice full of emotion. "Is there any hope for me?"

Alicia turned, her moist eyes sparkling like diamonds. "Oh, yes, yes," she whispered, her expression full of joy and adoration. "I love you, too."

"Oh, my darling," his lordship cried out, crushing her to him. "My Aphrodite, my goddess of love, this time I will never let you go."

"Nor I, you," she replied, raising her arms around his neck as he lowered his head and captured her lips with his own in a kiss which seemed to fuse their souls as well as their future.

If you would like to receive details on other Walker Regency romances, please write to:

The Regency Editor
Walker and Company
720 Fifth Avenue
New York, New York 10019